The Exceptional Exception

The Exceptional Exception

JOANN V. ALTIERO

RESOURCE *Publications* · Eugene, Oregon

THE EXCEPTIONAL EXCEPTION

Resource Publications
An Imprint of Wipf and Stock Publishers
199 W. 8th Ave., Suite 3
Eugene, OR 97401

www.wipfandstock.com

PAPERBACK ISBN: 978-1-6667-3404-1
HARDCOVER ISBN: 978-1-6667-2947-4
EBOOK ISBN: 978-1-6667-2948-1

01/19/22

I dedicate this book to the memory of my dear husband, Robert, who brought love and joy into my life.

May God embrace you as you enter the joys of heaven.

For those who wish to accept miracles,
laugh and cry,
open up this story's gift of love
to become part of a special cadre of seekers
who may be the Exceptional Exception
ALTIERO, 2021

Contents

Preface   *ix*

Chapter One: The Awakening   1

Chapter Two: Getting What Is Needed, Not Wanted   16

Chapter Three: Thy Will Be Done   22

Chapter Four: Casting Stones   25

Chapter Five: Suffering as a Gift   30

Chapter Six: Mercy   34

Chapter Seven: Faith and Courage   38

Chapter Eight: Creationism   42

Chapter Nine: The Eyes and Ears of the Soul   44

Chapter Ten: Reflections of God's Love   48

Chapter Eleven: The Mystery of Forgiveness   52

Chapter Twelve: Divine Providence in Forgiveness   57

Chapter Thirteen: God's Comforting Bird Poop!   66

Chapter Fourteen: Faith   69

Chapter Fifteen: A Calling from God   72

Chapter Sixteen: A Nun's Friendship   74

Chapter Seventeen: What to Do with a Gift from God?   76

Chapter Eighteen: The Parable   78

Chapter Nineteen: My Mary Magdalene   81

Chapter Twenty: The Paraclete   85

Chapter Twenty-One: Original Sin   93

Chapter Twenty-Two: Highly Sensitive, Purity of Heart   97

Chapter Twenty-Three: Angry at God   99

Chapter Twenty-Four: My Best Friend   101

Chapter Twenty-Five: Love One Another as I Have Loved You   103

Chapter Twenty-Six: You Have Forgotten How Much I Love You!   107

Chapter Twenty-Seven: Lessons of Love   115

Chapter Twenty-Eight: In the Park   118

Preface

"In the silence of my heart.
I think of you oh Lord."
ALTIERO, 1998

The truth is elementary. God is divine love, undefinable by words or by the beauty of this earth or even by angels' celestial songs. However, the more we love, the more we know God. We live life to experience this love and to learn that love is a choice. Free will distinguishes us from other living and created things. The opportunity to choose affords us an option to love, which begins the process of aligning our will to God's will, whether we know his benevolent intention or not.

This book deals with love and God through the story of Teresa. Teresa, a mystic, embarks on a marvelous journey to answer age-old philosophical questions while witnessing the supernatural in the natural setting of a park. As she struggles to align her will with God's, Teresa finds herself in a problematic quandary regarding the many souls who appear to be lost. Teresa soon discovers that we are all lost little sheep, running amok, looking for meaning or happiness in our lives.

Some look to addictions to fill their spiritual void or longing. They unknowingly restrict their freedom by pursuing drugs, alcohol, work, power, or prestige. Desires entrap and surround them as if in a cage by metal bars. They desperately rattle their self-made prison while in search of a key. Enticements of the senses are alluring. This activity might work for a while, but the feeling of satisfaction is only temporary; it is an illusion, a wrong turn in the dark that ends in the blackness of despair. Oddly, people keep going down this dark tunnel because it is familiar—not because it is correct. Some may suggest this pattern is an example of lazy thinking or simply not knowing any other way. Teresa wonders whether there is another way.

Teresa finds that there is another way. She has a spiritual awakening one day as her soul is touched gently by a mystical experience. Teresa falls into a state of humility, which leaves her full of questions rather than sure of answers. Her soul is searching earnestly, and she feels incomplete. Teresa plummets into a night of the soul. During the peak of her frustration, she meets a bedraggled older man in the park. After venturing along some paths that lead to dead ends, Teresa realizes that the self-righteous dogmas of hardened hearts are sterile; the rules people make to feel superior to others or to control others are traps. Instead, the truth resides in the vision of belonging to God's family and the liberating act of eternal love. Through divine mercy, we are responsible to one another, and we are capable of the most beautiful, valuable example of our humanness—the precious, priceless act of love. Through God's story, we experience what is beyond ourselves and the essence of our soul.

Teresa is familiar with the precious, priceless acts of gratuitous love since they were given to her early in her life. She receives gracious gifts throughout her life that reveal to her the absolute joy of her soul. By understanding the soul's beauty and exploring the spirit's actual capacity, Teresa becomes aware that people are much more than their physical bodies.

Teresa's insight and achievement are not so easy; a person must accept the possibility of having a soul. To achieve this end—to "ping" the soul—one must experience divine love and the soul. One shares the multiple facets of divine love in their depth and beauty and discovers the reason for our existence. To accept that another part of ourselves exists that we cannot see (i.e., the soul) might sound either ludicrous or frightening. I mean, the idea that part of us is hovering around, undetected like a stealth bomber, can be a bit daunting! Fortunately, as you will see, Teresa is both passionate and bold.

People could go in circles, pondering the existence of the soul and worrying about alternate realities, but what purpose would that serve? The literature is rife with idle speculations on these subjects, and I have read some excellent books. However, why not also think about the simple truth? What does love have to do with it? Many come to know love or to know God through experience and the softening of their hearts. Suffering forces empathy training, unknown to many; it is a gift. Our life events continue to act profoundly as a finger pointing to the soul's presence, and those who wait for a miracle are missing the big one—the single act of love. This act of love demonstrates that we are all here together, waiting for the beauty to unfold.

A saint or theologian does not write this book. Instead, it is the work of a sinner involved in the hazards and even the casualties of life. These quirks and mistakes that we make—you, Teresa, and I—are often regretted by the end of the day. Through a book about the soul's presence, by a sinner and mere mortal, let us try to make sense of the chaos in our lives. Teresa's story touches the essence of the soul. Her story is also God's story, which shows us what is beyond ourselves. His endless, magnificent act of merciful love allows us to share this reality beyond and to investigate the face of that which is indescribable: his divine mercy. So, we begin with stories of love and discussions about the essence of our souls.

This book is about love, its importance in our lives, and love's impact on the lives of others. We follow a single soul, Teresa, on her mystical journey toward a beautiful awareness of the human soul and the endless mystery of God. Until Teresa discovers divine providence, the series of events within her life appears chaotic, lacking in order, meaning, or reason. Yet, she continues to search, sometimes with angry obstinacy. However, while searching for the truth, she finds her imperfections, creating heavy sorrow within her heart.

Nevertheless, she perseveres, awakening the wisdom that is available to all of us. For it is during our weakness that we are vital due to the gift of humility. Teresa also learns not to be so hard on herself, because such behavior focuses on the love of self rather than God. Fortunately, out of relentless effort, she discovers a beautiful treasure within herself and others. Will you take this journey with her to this stunning discovery? Love never ends, and your life is a magnificent journey toward the discovery of his great secret. I love you, and I pray God protects you.

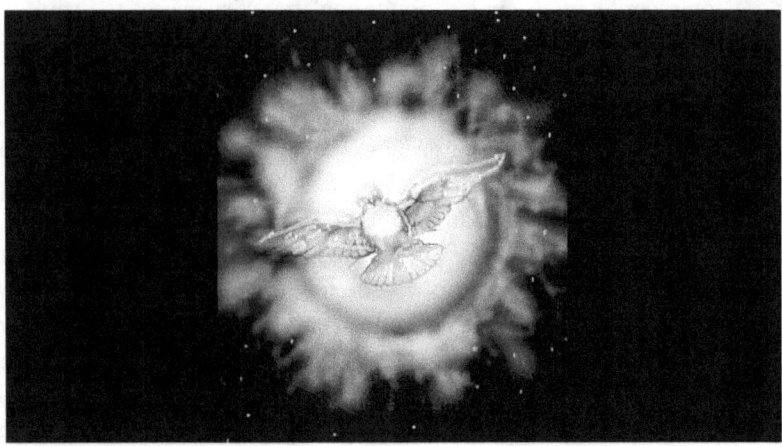

Anyone can become a mystic like Teresa; everyone has the potential to discover an intimate relationship with God. Very little courage on the part of each humble soul can propel one into a magnificent journey back home to the origin before time and space.

Chapter One

The Awakening

"To love him is to know him,
To know him is to love him"
ALTIERO, 1998

The sun streams through the clouds, cascading yellow ribbons on a gift of blue sky. A woman pauses to smile before she enters the park—another gorgeous day. A school of finches, their wings fluttering on a nearby bush, applaud the thistle's beauty, topped by a brilliant array of butterflies rejoicing heavenward. Always prepared, the peculiar woman wears an olive hiker's hat securely attached under her chin. The hat is a bit bedraggled due to wear, matching the wrinkles about her curious eyes, which have character and a story to tell. She has some water, sunscreen, and bug repellent to complete the entire seven miles. She is a frequent visitor at the park that people are driving by waving with a smile or snicker.

Teresa is drawn to the park and has been hiking there for years. Nature offers a perpetual symphony of colors and sounds throughout the seasons. A butterfly lightly taps her nose with a cheerful welcome. Two cardinals swoop low into the trees right beside her and magically disappear within the cover of the red fall leaves. "I know you are there," Teresa whispers. Both cardinals are devoted followers of the mysterious hiker and begin their serenade. Teresa is courteous and gently replies, "Thank you, my loves!" The birds take flight ahead of her to lead the way. It is incredible how every hike in the park can offer a new adventure. It is astounding to think that the most awesome spectacles play out here like a movie, with multiple encores, at no cost.

Teresa has always felt tremendous gratitude toward God for creating nature and attributes the gift to God's benevolence. However, lately, something appears to be changing within Teresa during her walks. She finds herself glorifying and thanking God for even the smallest detail of each monarch butterfly, and she feels at these times a connection she has not felt before. Charming munificence streaming toward her from God suggests that he delights in her enjoyment.

"Does everyone enjoy your gifts as I do?" Teresa wonders. Through exalted experiences of this kind, Teresa is growing keenly aware of her soul's existence, which brings such delight that she can hardly think. Even more astounding, the animals are mindful of what is going on as she joins them in some secret mystery. Indeed, in turn, Teresa feels a closeness to the spirit of animals and all creation, giving forth the glory of God. She perceives God as a generous father who loves to spend time with his children. His kindness and generosity often bring Teresa to tears, even though she cannot return to her Father what he directs toward his children.

Teresa feels entirely alone, at times, although so remarkably close to her loving Father. She feels separate from the world and other people—very vulnerable as when in love. How could a soul share such experiences with others if they do not experience the soul's awakening?

One day, while walking in the park, remembering her childhood, Teresa cannot forget some troubling and unusual experiences. When another person witnesses the event and testifies to the occasion, it is fortunate, as happened on that night. Teresa recalls being in her room with her cousin Carla, who was about age eight at the time, one year older than Teresa. The light in the night sky draws them both to the window. Is it a floodlight or a car headlight? No, it is emitting from a supernatural source in the sky—to the amazement of both girls.

A delicate glow appears in the night sky; the street is empty and dark below. Gasping, they draw closer to the window. The light, increasingly intensive, is coming right toward both girls. Vivid white wings extend beyond the brilliant central light source—not frightening but excellent. As the beautiful vision comes directly through the window, it soars straight into Teresa's chest. Carla's face shifts from amazement to shock, "I saw the light, it got bigger, and there was a dove. It went into your chest, Teresa! Where did it go?"

For years, the memory persists, and there are times when Teresa's analytical mind claims the best of her regarding the mysterious event from their childhood. A double hallucination called *folie à deux* could occur if just one person is insane. As a teenager, Teresa watches her cousin closely to see if she can detect signs of psychosis. If not Carla, would it be Teresa who is crazy? As they grow older, they cannot deny that it happened. When Carla goes to medical school, she is deemed unequivocally sane. Teresa is afraid of herself: It must be me! Finally, during Teresa's doctoral training, the day of the dreaded self-evaluation arrives. Indeed, that will reveal the awful truth. So, she scribbles and erases, shaking her head as if doomed. A peer looks up and giggles at Teresa's seriousness with the task. Teresa looks at the woman in desperation as if hiding a terrible secret. The woman, Joya, laughs and cajoles her to be calm. "Joya, great. The day I find out I am the nut case, and you are laughing."

Before Joya can respond with more soothing words, the department director interrupts to explain that it is okay to have some elevations. "Obtaining higher scores on the scales for schizophrenia or histrionic personality may suggest a bit of creativity or a pleasant, outgoing personality."

"I will take some of that," Teresa thinks. "Well, unfortunately, I am not out for lunch, and this is not a smorgasbord." Oddly, she turns out to be low on every scale except obsessive-compulsive, suggesting that she may tend to worry. No kidding! She needs a form to tell her that. "Look, Joya, I am just a boring bookworm. Well, at least that is safe. I have something new to worry about. I can kill someone with boredom."

"I am not dead."

"Well, Joya, you don't know me well enough yet."

Teresa begins to worry about being obsessive. The program director then says to the forty adults in the room, "Did anyone get a little high on the obsessive-compulsive scale?" Teresa raises her hand, as does the other fellowship recipient.

"You two are likely the only two that will make it through the program."

Well, Teresa is sure she will find some reason to worry. Like all the other students that she kills off with boredom. Poor Joya! Joya is studying her with a severe, worried expression. She has put her glasses on to create a dramatic effect that makes Teresa laugh aloud.

"I have a little histrionic tendency, which is dazzling, isn't it?"

"Yes, it is, and I love you for it, Joya—just what I need to get off my pity-pot."

Teresa, from then on, accepting the mystical experience of her childhood for what it is, frequently begins to call on that mysterious light, that visitor from her early days. Her dove friend—a sage, the great comforter—is always with her. As she gets older, she acknowledges the dove as the Holy Spirit.

Not all of Teresa's experiences have been delightful; shortly afterward, another visit from the light came into a frightening dream. Teresa was seven years old at the time. Upon falling asleep, one night, she finds herself in total darkness. This blackness is blacker than black. If she closes her eyes and opens them again, it is much darker. How frightening. What is that? Who is that? Teresa can hear a tremor in her voice, revealing her fear of the invisible presence, an unidentified thing in the black room. An authoritative voice crackles through the air, lacking human emotion. Shocking Teresa's body with rivets of pain amuses the presence. With each jolt of electrical current, he yells at Teresa, "Deny your love of God. Deny your love of God!" Teresa senses utter hopelessness in a dark place—a netherworld. She is searching for the flame of hope for the faithful: the love of God to light the way.

Teresa does not understand why the mysterious adult is treating her in this way and telling her to do something wrong. How can she respect him, even though he is an elder? There is something very wrong here, something very wrong. The scary person shocks her again and states, "You deny your love of God, or I will torture you and take you down to the netherworld with me for all eternity." A netherworld is a place of terrible darkness. Where can Teresa put her hope? She needs just a little flame in the dark. The love of God will light the way!

"I am sad when I think of a place full of darkness," Teresa reflects. "Yet, I know if I take with me my little flame, my love of God, I can hold a tiny flame in the dark, and that will be my love of God, however small."

Teresa now responds to the tempter. "Then take me down to the netherworld for all eternity, but I will not deny my love of God. For if I did, it would be better if I had never been born!" The evil entity does not expect this courageous response. Aghast, while retreating, the hideous creature emits a bloodcurdling scream. The deep howl is like the sound of a wounded beast, cast into a bottomless, dark pit and falling into the hopeless despair of its hatred.

How could such a small child, meek and innocent, make an unexpectedly piercing response toward an ancient, evil entity? By the sound of his hissing, the tempter experiences a fatal wound. Innocence is demolishing his relentless pride by a steadfast blow of faith and hope. A bolt of purity, light sent toward the toxic, evil entity, casts out his putrid form. A pure white light, whiter than white, enters the room—a familiar and peaceful presence.

With the comforting light comes a wise voice, gentle and reassuring. "That is the master of deceit, the prince of all lies." Following his ominous forewarning words came a protective reassurance that she did well. "I only told the truth. I have to have hope," she thinks. He has no hope, but she does not feel sorry for him. That entity is not of God. He is no part of God. God has no interest in that hopeless creature who hates children—nor does she. For she wills to love God with her entire mind, heart, strength, and soul.

Teresa, now a professional woman, has been working for numerous years with children and adults. She finds it all quite unbelievable—not just the event itself but also her response at such an early age. In the park, during her walk, the sun is now blinding her view. So, she uses her hand as a visor to find the nearest bench. She continues to reflect on the past. At such an early age, how did a child produce such wisdom? A bumblebee buzzes by Teresa's ear, bringing her back to the present. She flaps her hand to usher the bee away. "Where did you come from, little bee?" Teresa regains her focus, again remembering the oddity of her childhood. A young girl, just age seven, responds to a frightening entity with dedication, truth, and honesty. Her eloquent words can be attributed to the wisdom of the dove from her vision the previous year.

To revisit her childhood and assess her early adulthood helps make sense of where Teresa now stands as she approaches retirement. Divine providence or the hand of God is visible—as clear as the baby blue sky above her head, where a bald eagle soars blissfully, with direction and strength.

Though she has experienced numerous mysterious events, Teresa questions their spiritual validity. Truthfully, it has only been through great suffering that Teresa has acquired the potential to accept her soul's existence and her mystical experiences as spiritually relevant. Finally, her pain opened the door to mysticism and landed her back on the intended journey.

Often during her most despairing moments of childhood, Teresa could feel that familiar, uplifting presence nearby, reminding her of the comforter. Though the evil one might still be angry at her, she could trust the comforter's guidance and lean on the divine presence. Ah, someone to trust and lean on! Earlier, as a teenager, she is led to the Son of God. Now, while walking in the park, so many years later, Teresa's heart beats a little faster in anticipation. Could that entirely trustworthy person be nearby?

Teresa has always thirsted for God. She constantly has conversations with someone worthy of perfect trust. She trusts the eyes and ears of her soul, the soul's senses, since she cannot see or hear God's son with the eyes and ears of her body. The Lord requires sincerity of heart and a committed desire for the truth. Who should she trust for spiritual direction? A trustworthy person is truthful, with integrity, and desires not to harm you. This person has competency, true wisdom. Ideally, we may find someone with a perfect heart and perfect competency in knowing the truth when seeking spiritual guidance. When obtaining such requirements in a spiritual advisor, rather than a failing mortal, it is an incredible blessing—if met by a sacred human, the son of God.

"Jesus, can I acquire perfect trust?" she wonders. "I know that perfect faith will be a challenge." Jesus makes a great friend, and he is reassuring. He is patient and maintains an exquisite sense of humor, which is a comfort to Teresa because she can be silly. One day when she enters the park after a heavy rain, for instance, her shoes fill with water. "My Lord, how will I learn about perfect trust if I fear my shoes fill with water?"

The Lord responds, "What? You don't like to walk on water?"

Teresa, caught off guard, breaks into a hysterical fit of laughter in the company of the Son of Man, telling jokes.

"I didn't know you were so funny!" He looks at her like as if she is making a peculiar statement. Teresa realizes her faux pas and quickly corrects it. "I am sorry, Lord, I forgot you invented humor, too. Well, it wasn't in the Bible, so unless there is poor editing . . ."

"Reread it, and you will find it."

Contemplative mystics often receive information to which the public is not privy. The Bible can hold just so many stories. Upon contemplation, stories can and do evolve. The Bible is the living truth.

THE STORY OF PETER

One of Teresa's favorite stories is the one shared about Saint Peter when he was a child. Teresa listens through the ears of the soul as the Lord recounts the story.

"Teresa, Peter and his father are pretty close. My father and I share much enjoyment remembering the love between these two. Peter and his father, Jonah, both enjoy fishing. He was a large, muscular man when his son was small, for age seven. Nevertheless, Peter will not miss this time with his father for the world. He so loves him, and we love them. They get up early in the morning before the sun lights up the sky and the twinkling stars say their farewell to the night. Peter will help his father, Jonah, prepare the nets as they both pray; first, prayers of gratitude and then requests that they catch many fish."

While passing by the pond at the park, Teresa looks at the reflection in the water, expecting to see fish, but instead, she only sees the tops of the trees. A bullfrog jumps up with a baritone ribbit and causes her unexpectedly to laugh. Teresa dutifully apologizes to the Lord, "Did anything unusual happen that morning with Jonah and his son?"

The Lord continues, "When Jonah yells, 'Fish!' Peter jumps, up unable to contain his excitement, and almost loses his footing, nearly toppling over. His father says, 'Sit down, Peter! You will topple out of the boat. Do you want to drown?' Peter gives his father a giant smile and obediently sits down. Minutes later, Jonah says, 'Wow, a great catch,' and Peter pops up. Again, he says, 'Sit down, Peter! You will topple out of the boat. Do you want to drown?' Finally, Jonah tugs up a massive lot of fish, and Peter pops up. Then for the third time, Jonah says, 'Sit down, Peter! You will topple out of the boat. Would you want to drown?'

"On that last word, to Jonah's horror, Peter loses his balance and topples straight out of the boat and into the sea. His son goes straight down to the bottom, causing Jonah to drop the net, losing his day's catch, because nothing means more to Jonah than his boy. He quickly dives into the water, praying, 'Please, Lord, take my life and not my son's!' He sees a tiny arm flailing in front of him and grabs his son's hand. He pulls him up to the boat by the scruff of his neck. Peter looks terrified while coughing out water and gasping for air. Jonah says, 'Three times, Peter, three times I told you not to stand up.' Then he looks at the terror in his son's face and remembers the horror he felt seconds ago. He smiles at his son and says, 'Ha! This morning I thought I was a fisher of fish, not a fisher of men.' Peter can smile and can accept a hug from his beloved father."

After the Lord finishes the story, Teresa asks, "Are you saying that Peter, although having a frightful childhood experience, is the same Peter who dared to come to you when you walked on water? Oh no! He sank then too."

The Lord reminds Teresa that his hand was there just as his father's hand was, and love was the way. "Love is always there, whether you know it or not."

Teresa comments, "He also denied you three times. You also asked him three times if he loved you. Jesus? Jesus?" But Jesus is not there. It appears that Jesus has left for the day, according to his occasional custom.

Sometimes people catch Teresa talking to the animals or a friend that is not there, gesturing with her hands and nodding as if in response to an invisible presence. Some people passing by give a smile and nod of understanding, while others back away, producing a quick diagnosis. Teresa loves the Lord's stories so much. Sometimes Teresa wants to see Jesus with her eyes and yet feels ashamed of that desire. Jesus would say to her soul, "I am here. You know I am here." Though she might plead for quite a long time, Teresa would finally give up her whining. Surely, she needs to develop some virtues of character. Once her character is pure, will it be easier to see the Lord directly?

One day, upon entering the park, she feels an eerie absence. Something is off. Has she done something wrong? She looks behind her. An incomprehensible sorrow overcomes her—alone and in the dark. Where is he? The storyteller?

"Why aren't you here?" Teresa asks aloud.

She startles the couple behind her, who query, "Are you talking to us?"

"No, I am sorry," Teresa responds quickly. What a severe lesson. Suddenly her hope darkens and vanishes. The light inside appears to be snuffed out abruptly like the flame of a candle. Tears well up in Teresa's eyes. Then she becomes furious. "I trusted you! I trusted you," she rages. This attack of rage and desperation lasts an entire day. This night of the soul lasts three consecutive days. The lone walker travels many miles to the point of exhaustion. She punishes herself, reflecting harshly on all her mistakes in life and all she has taken for granted. Crossing a road to Damascus, all certainty is lost. On the road to Damascus, the wanderer stumbles and falls, neither once nor twice, but much more often.

"Sometimes, when I glance behind me," Teresa observes, "I see many marks on the soil where I lose my footing. Those dark prints represent the colors of my sinfulness. They are fading images as the noonday sun passes over my head; the mercy of God, who is accounting for my sins, is felt by my sorrowful heart. The accounting by human standards measures the depth of my fall by the shadow of darkness: my sinfulness, the darkness of my soul, peers back at me in the night. Out of the void within, a gaping hole arises strenuous questioning: Why? Why? I do not know why I have been given so much and done so little. I could have done more, would have done more, if not for my wretched sinfulness. As I glance behind me, I see fewer mishaps and falls earlier in the journey because the Lord has taken pity on me as a neophyte by sending angels and comforters as guides. I had more courage then, every day was a consolation, and the joy and tenderness of his love came to me through multiple miracles due to the grace of faith. Now I am alone, without the comforts of my youth, without the consolations from my

Lord. Jesus, whom I hold so close to my heart, is missing I can choose to love. Yet in the silence of my heart, I cry to you, oh Lord!"

On the second day, it is difficult to return to the park. She has not slept well and has numerous reasons not to go, but she does go. A storm has covered the park while she has struggled with sleep. Was the thunder loud due to God's anger at his ungrateful children? Many tree branches are hanging off trees; some are splitting. The broken trees appear to bow in the sky like sorrowful, penitent sinners, joining this vagabond who has not even run a brush through her hair. Teresa walks all day in desperation with intermittent misery and exhaustion. "Where have you gone, my Love?" she calls. A dove sings a coo of sorrows. Teresa continues, thirsting, considering: "My feet are dirty, covered with sand and dust from my travels. I am in dry land without water. Where is the well? Will I perish in a desert of heat and dust? Am I just a speck of dust floating upon a voice of uncertainty and diminishing into silence? My throat is dry and coarse. I cough to clear the sand, which does nothing to improve my condition."

The sun is setting. The stars rise in the heavens like glistening tears. She has walked so far for so long that the park is almost empty. A couple of foxes come out startled by her presence before running back to their dens.

"It is so tranquil; all I can hear is the sound of my soul, like the grunt of an old horse, and the clop, clop of hoofs, no longer carrying my weight but just provisions for the evening. You see, my soul is thirsty and afraid because I am losing my place in existence, just as a warm desert wind blows and the sun sets. Is there a purpose to this suffering? A fitful sleep besets me, the wary traveler. Will I be the only soul in purgatory?"

A raccoon looks at her on the path as he clutches a partial sandwich left by a picnicker, ready to challenge Teresa if she tries to grab the loot from his recent theft. Like a masked bandit, he will lend her his mask so that she can hide when she gets to purgatory. Alas, the cover is attached, so the raccoon scampers off. Exhausted, disappointed by the raccoon, she turns toward a passing car as passengers yell at her. "The Park is closed; you should leave!" Other passers-by add denigrating remarks in mocking tones.

Teresa is reflecting on life after death and her fate. "People will find it surprising that such a common type does not make it into heaven with everyone else. Why? I cause no one great harm and even help a few. Nevertheless, I have been given much and have done extraordinarily little.

"For this reason, this soul is to receive great humiliation because all who know will look at me, this solitary soul, with great pity. I stand before them all with great shame but realize that even this shame is good for my soul because, through such suffering, I may acquire some humility. Again, a gift that I cannot repay in any way! The soul cries shrouded in the darkness.

Will a whispering wind awaken me? Will a soft voice float into the silence of the night below the sparkling stars? Will the Prince of Peace whisper, 'You have forgotten how much I love you?'"

Teresa is waiting and hears nothing. Yet here again is the raccoon. He has completed his sandwich and looks at her as if she might join him in his next heist. "No, little Robby the raccoon, I think I have committed plenty of sins for a lifetime. You have an enjoyable time." With that, he takes off into the bush.

The next day Teresa arises with trepidation and determination, an incongruous combination of qualities. That is Teresa, a set of contradictions. Someone has cleaned up the wastage from the previous night's storm and turmoil. Some small trees timidly lift their heads and foliage, grasping at the sun as it welcomes the new day. Teresa addresses God as she looks at the tree. "I, too, will relinquish control. It is not like I can stop loving you because you are such a part of me now. Just as the little tree lifts its head in the hope of sun, I too will do so."

On the third day, Teresa enters further into the park. The silence is still as if loud. The couple who startled her three days before is there. Without looking up with her usual friendly smile, she states sullenly, addressing her imaginary beloved friend, "I just need to know, have you forsaken me?" The couple warily hurries by her and wave at an older man, whom they pass. The man is sitting on a park bench.

Mike and Maggie are a married couple with numerous inquisitive children. Although pleased with their children's intellectual understanding, they need a daily break from all their questions. Mike and Maggie often observe Teresa in the park mumbling, and they attribute her preoccupied behavior to a blue tooth device connected to her phone. However, today the couple notice that she is listening neither to a phone nor music. The woman seems to be talking to someone who is not there—somewhat puzzling, neither happy nor content. She looks friendly and harmless, however, regardless of her creative tendencies and eccentricities. This couple has many parenting experiences, having tolerated numerous quirks from adorable children who love their imaginary friends.

"Some people just don't grow out of their self-directed speech," Maggie whispers to Mike.

Mike does not miss a beat. "Hold up, Maggie! I am talking to my higher self, and you are interrupting our conversation." The comment strikes Maggie as hysterically funny—as Mike is often amusing—and his humor is just enough to relieve Maggie's concerns about the lone hiker, who is now approaching a bench in the far distance.

ON THE BENCH

Teresa usually sits on the bench to check her miles on her tracker. How annoying that an older adult is sitting in the middle seat of "her" bench. She has
not slept well for three days. The old guy looks a bit unkempt, he is a cranky
man, and she does not look forward to his response when she asks him to
move his grubby self over so that she can share the bench. Is this man homeless? Has he slept on the seat the night before? Vagrants are often hauled off
in the middle of the night by the park police—could this be one of them?

Teresa is irritated and has multiple justifications about why anyone
who has experienced her disappointments need not justify behaving like a
snot. The older man, who sees Teresa approaching, leans on his black cane
to scoot over. There is now space for Teresa to sit down. Without an appreciation for his gesture, Teresa thinks, "What if he is a dirty older man, or
he stinks?"

Teresa continues her belittling rant inside her head. "He has got this
Albert Einstein appearance going on but likely not a thought in his old gray
head. He will probably talk nonstop about all his physical ailments, which
he believes are somewhat impressive."

Teresa considers quite a few more nasty things, but finally, her passionate tirade dies down, and she flops onto the bench. She looks at him. He
looks at her. Then he looks away with a deep sigh.

Teresa grunts, "Oh, here it comes, and now he's going to say something
like, 'Oh, my Brontosaurus bone is killing me!'" And she will have to say,
"No, it's not! That is a dinosaur bone, you idiot, and you do not have one!
You are as old as the dinosaurs, but you don't have one." The older man looks
over at Teresa again, as if comprehending the snarl—and then looks away.

Suddenly, like a sword to Teresa's stomach, there arises a familiar pang
of guilt due to her excessive temper. What has Jesus said? "Whatsoever you
do to the least of my brothers that you do unto me." Teresa rolls her eyes
at this reminder. "Oh no! Crap!" This experience must be a test, and she is
failing miserably, disappointing the Lord. Grimacing, Teresa queries herself.
How could she ever expect to see him, her Lord, with so much nasty stuff
in her personhood?

Now Teresa whimpers; the tears start to flow. Suddenly, she blurts out,
"I am sorry, Mister, I am having a horrible day!" He turns to look at her, and
although she is relieved by the sadness and kindness in his eyes, she also
feels more guilty.

He asks her, "What is wrong?"

Maybe Mr. Kind Eyes can help. "I don't want to bother you. I am so rude. I did not even thank you for moving over. I do not deserve your kindness."

The man smiles, claiming he knows many children and grandchildren that have their days too. That day, Teresa opens a floodgate.

"In some way, I feel like Judas, the apostle, a tragic victim of hopelessness due to his lack of trust in God. I accept what he gives but not what he takes away. My friend, with his beautiful stories, I am so selfish! This lack of confidence in God is the beast's signature. Expelled from heaven due to disobedience and relentless doubts, that master of deceit, the prince of all lies, vents his fury throughout the ages. That which is darker than black hates—and we are hated. Even so, we are magnificent and majestic creatures because God loves us so much. I don't know why, and I don't understand why God loves us so, and it often makes me cry."

Teresa swallows hard. She notices a praying mantis standing on her shoe, looking more out of place than she feels. Teresa slightly moves her foot to see if it will jump off, but the creature just looks at her with its large beady eyes, hanging on for dear life. Teresa continues her lament.

"I then get demanding, insisting that I should get what I want and when I want it. I make up rules as to why this should be so. Just like Saul, who thought there should be rules to control others. What do I want to control God to do? We usually do not do well because we are foolish. I know that I am. In these last three days, I had traveled the road to Damascus with Saul before he was reborn as Paul. I am looking for my Lord at every turn so foolishly."

The older man's eyes widen, and he turns toward her, showing his great interest. Teresa notes that, amidst the wrinkles of his right eye, there are delightful freckles. His unruly hair, primarily white gray, is fragile and would blow back with the slightest wind. There is a depth in his eyes that she has not noted before. His greeting is so pleasant and accepting. Such a supportive and kind gentleman, might he have been sent to her by the comforter? Her best friend, Jesus, has gone missing after a lifetime of consultations. Yet, here sits a compassionate listener, instead. We may not get what we want, but we receive what we need.

Without removing his eyes from Teresa, the older man takes a piece of straw from his front pocket. He chews on the tip while gesturing for her to continue.

The praying mantis is still on Teresa's shoe.

Teresa continues speaking of holy things. "The sin of having too much is that we then want too much. The crime of wanting too much is that we lose our gratitude toward the father. An overattachment to this world's things or spiritual comforts often causes a burden to our souls. We need a mule to help us carry all our garbage. The devotion to lesser things creates a barrier to our union with God. This truth holds. Instead, one can be grateful for the opportunity to love God and the potential to love God increasingly, as long as the breath of life is within us."

Then Teresa turns to speak to the praying mantis, "Hey, if you are planning on getting a free ride on my shoe, you better keep praying for me!" The praying mantis jumps up onto her lap, causing both the older man and Teresa to chuckle. She lets it stay on her knee to continue its prayers.

Teresa speaks now again to the older adult. "Peace begins in the heart; it is found only through gratefulness toward our awesome God. God's power is endless, and it is to be feared. God's mercy is mysterious and different from human compassion. God's love is endless, unlike our passion, often investing only in our human estate. There is too much in paradise. Sin creeps in where we want even more. Adam and Eve ate the apple with greed. In demanding what we want and not accepting what we need, we lose our gratitude toward the Father (the will is no longer cooperative with God). Since God is awesome, we do well to fear and trust God. God's mercy and God's love are infinite gifts beyond our understanding, even though I miss my Jesus terribly."

The older man is now nodding. He asks, "Have you ever thought about Jesus on the cross when he cries out, 'Abba, why have you abandoned me?'" The praying mantis tilts its head from side to side as if to say, "Well, have you?" Now, Teresa senses something very unusual about the insect but decides to answer the question.

Teresa has thought deeply about the private, mystical moment between Father and Son, which often confuses people. So, she replies. "Why would Jesus, Son of God, cry out to God with such despair? 'Abba! Father!' Why? We often do not understand because we are foolish people. During our lives, when we suffer, we often feel that our God is distant and far away. Later we realize that God was there. We just did not know it. Yes, consciously, we did not feel it, but our soul knew the truth and presence of God regardless of our denial. It is hubris to believe that Jesus felt something similar on the cross.

"That moment of separation is unlike what we will ever actually feel as humans. During the private conversation between the loving Father and his son, God reveals that his passion will save the people he loves endlessly from a horrible abandonment. As his sheep, humans will never experience the total horror of separation from God, as the evil one has for eternity. Separation is a break that includes our consciousness, feelings, and the soul. Only Jesus knows what it is; the last horror was the final and most severe in his sorrowful and selfless passion. We will not know what it is to be separated from all sources of love and abandoned to a darkness blacker than black, where demons live in total despair and hopelessness. If our spirit separates from God, we will cease to exist as a soul. The ripping away of our souls from God is a pain not comparable to any suffering in human existence—even that of physical death.

"The blood of Jesus spares us. On the cross, painful gifts are exchanged between Father and Son. God has accepted the suffering of Jesus for the people, his sheep, whom he loves endlessly, and God has spared us from that horrific moment. Finally, in sweet sorrow and gratitude, the love of my life bows his head and says, 'It is finished.' In Latin, *per crucem et Passionem tuam, Libera nos Domine, domine.* By Your Cross and Passion, Deliver us, Lord, Lord. Amen."

A tear falls from Teresa's eyes as she speaks.

The older man's patient response is noteworthy because most people shut her down when she talks about her great love for the master of her heart. The older man has a sparkle in his eye and does not rebuke her faith at all. Although Teresa still suffers from a wounded heart due to her special friend's absence, this older gentleman has made the pain quite bearable, as if he has lifted a heavy cross from her shoulder—with his compassionate gaze and attentive manner. The sun appears to be shining today more brightly in the park. Teresa's burden is light. The lines and folds within the man's forehead and eyes mark a meaningful history of listening to others. The praying mantis jumps on the older man's shoulder to listen to Teresa, too.

Teresa mostly talks, and the man attentively listens. On occasion, an animal shows up to act peculiarly. Such events cause them to giggle. Unless, of course, an aggressive jaybird shows up. Today the jaybird warns of his coming by a scream while landing on a branch. He hurries to one side and yells at them and then meanders to the other side to cry some more. Teresa is appalled by his aggression, but the older man laughs and laughs. Oh, how Teresa loves his laugh! She cannot remember when she laughed so much. A little squirrel, observing their conversation, runs up to the bench with an acorn. The excited bushy-tailed animal places the meal down as an offering before the two are involved in their conversation. How odd is it for an animal to give food up, or is the curious rug rat telling them they are nuts?

Teresa returns to their previous conversation. "So, you see, I feel a bit lost!"

The older man responds with comforting words. "Oh, you lost little lamb!"

The squirrel returns and grabs the nut he has left behind due to their lack of gratitude; undoubtedly, both Teresa and the older man laugh knowingly, for the curious animal is also hungry.

There is a tear on the shoulder of the man's tweed jacket. Have moths eaten it? Teresa decides she may bring a needle and thread to the park if needed and sew it for him.

"So, what did you do before you retired? I mean, I assume you have."

He smiles graciously. "I've never really retired. If you mean working to obtain payment, though, I am not receiving remuneration for my services. I do compose short stories or parables. I guess many people like them because they contain hidden lessons. They also like to discuss specific questions related to the stories."

What good fortune! Teresa has missed wise storytelling. It is when she stopped demanding and expecting something that she received. May the name of the Lord be praised! She blurts out, "Oh, please tell me one. Please! Please!"

The older adult smiles. "To have your attention, sweet child, of course, I will." He pauses and looks up at the sky, his hand on his chin, pondering and nodding his head. "I would like to tell you about Mr. Banks."

Chapter Two

Getting What Is Needed, Not Wanted

Bob Banks is a respected member of his community, a devoted family-oriented person, and successful at work. In fact, after many years of challenging work, Bob has acquired financial independence and great wealth. One frigid December morning, Bob calls for his chauffeur to pull up the limousine in front of his house because he is due to meet with a business partner early that morning. The air is so cold that the chauffeur's greeting ("Good morning!") hangs in the air like a frozen puff of smoke. Mr. Banks shivers as he reaches into his pockets for his gloves; he realizes that he has forgotten his scarf and, to his dismay, his gloves are missing. He must have left them on the counter inside. "Oh, well," Bob mutters. He is running late, so he lifts his expensive cashmere coat collar and hurries onto the warm seat of his awaiting limousine.

Mr. Banks wonders why God makes such frigid mornings like this one. This cold climate cannot be suitable for anyone, can it? Mr. Banks is quite sullen now. Why does God want him to suffer such a cold on a morning like this? Mr. Banks is just trying to provide for his family, and he gives generously at church. Why? Why? Why? Mr. Banks is still mulling over these concerns when they enter the city and come to a complete halt because of traffic congestion. Then, just by luck, he notices a movement out of the corner of his right eye. What is that? Turning, he catches sight of a homeless man who has rolled over onto a grate to obtain some heat from a building on the street. He is trying to cover himself with a newspaper because his filthy clothes are in tatters. Mr. Banks has passed such people numerous times in the past, people who want to warm themselves up in the dead of winter. The man is shivering.

Mr. Banks does not remember opening the door or why he feels compelled to jump out of the car. Doing so is automatic; he does not give it a thought. Suddenly, Bob Banks is removing his coat and wrapping the dirty man up in it! He is terrified that the man will indeed die in this cold. At first, the homeless man looks shocked, and then he starts to weep as the warmth returns to his body. Glistening tears of gratitude flow freely from a face adorned with creases of sorrow from suffering. The chauffeur steps out of the car in the middle of traffic, delightfully, to view the vagabond. His hopelessness is shattering.

Instead of the usual frantic city pace, pedestrians stop—many to ponder in wonder. Why is that wealthy man taking off his coat for that homeless man? Their curiosity brings the clanking of the mechanical city to a halt and point of silence. People collectively gather to gesture at the two men in amazement, and they are forming a crowd. They are unexpecting—the exceptional exception—inspiring cheers and whistles. The building crowd's applause is ebullient sounding from street to street. Their cries express the longing of humanity for beautiful gestures of kindness.

Kindness and mercy are welcome; they are eternally yearned for by all present within a very crowded street in Manhattan. The hug by two strangers sends waves of warmth throughout the city, which comes together like the extended family of God. The joy pouring into Mr. Banks overflows into a shared experience of brotherhood and sisterhood among all. With a nod, he acknowledges his lost brother. Then, as this incredible compassion expands his heart, Bob Banks saunters toward his car. Though shivering, he is feeling warmer than he ever has in his entire life! Mr. Banks arrives late for his meeting without a coat.

TALKING ABOUT MR. BANKS

The older man places both hands on his knees after finishing the story. He poses some questions for Teresa to consider. "What do you think was going on with Mr. Banks? Did he give the homeless man something more or other than a warm coat? What did each man learn about love if anything?"

Teresa furrows her brow with determination when responding, which makes her look severe and old but wise. She enjoys discussion. The older gentleman finds her face wondrous and joyful because her deep thinking indicates a virtue.

"I guess that people may have various opinions and, most likely, they are not all in agreement. Hopefully, people can respectfully resolve their differences of opinion better than I can. I guess some people may believe that Mr. Banks exhibited virtue, while others may think his gesture to be foolish. Some may argue that he would have contributed greater good by letting the homeless man meet his fate. Or he can sell his expensive coat and purchase multiple coats of modest price, in place of this one, and all of the coats can be a donation for the homeless." Teresa hopes to impress the teacher with her analytical ability. She leans forward to discover his expression. No, the teacher is not impressed; he looks bored. Teresa reflects that she is responding to the story analytically rather than spontaneously with the heart.

Now she speaks again, vigorously from the heart. "Wait a minute! Remember what Judas says when Mary of Bethany uses her hair and some expensive oil to bathe the feet of Jesus? Judas suggests that the oil is expensive and can be given to help the poor. Mr. Banks is like Mary, who anoints the feet of Jesus. Another consideration: Was the homeless man of a certain race, religion, or ethnicity? Does that matter? Jesus asks the Samaritan woman for water, although the ethnic customs of the day prohibited affiliation between Jews and Samaritans. Jesus crossed over those ethnic taboos. What about Mr. Banks? Well, he is an exciting fellow, all right."

Teresa takes the time to blow a bang off her forehead, which has wandered toward her eye. "Jesus always balances individual rights with the common good. Bob Banks has an awareness of community obligation, too, and a concern for human welfare. However, he goes farther that day. Why? On that frigid winter morning, he identifies with the man, personally, as an individual. A little suffering in the morning due to the cold opens the eyes of the soul. His slight sorrow turns into something beautiful. Life experience and sometimes suffering are required to acquire added dimensions of empathy and emotional maturity. Like Mr. Banks, we gain a collective sense of our place in the human family."

Now the bang has fallen back on her forehead, tickling her, and she pushes it away. The older man is slightly amazed by the bang fiasco. "Mr. Banks has a choice and the free will to make a decision. He may offer this suffering and use it for the glory of God. The torment of wintry weather works as a stimulus toward great virtue. Sometimes, we humans do need a swift kick in the pants. I know that I have often felt a more vital closeness to God and the love of Jesus within my suffering. Wait a minute! This story sounds like the tale of the good Samaritan."

The older man's eyes widened. "It does!"

"The good Samaritan must have suffered greatly and identified, personally, with the man who had fallen and lay beaten by the road. Jesus says, 'Whatever you do to the least of my brothers, you do unto me.' If Jesus comes alive through people because of suffering, then suffering is a gift. Mr. Banks and the homeless man are involved in the modern version of an old and classic story. It just goes to show. A delightful story will stand the test of time."

The older man acknowledges that a relevant story, presenting a sacred truth, is eternal. The gentleman speaks quite eloquently and seems curious about Teresa. In turn, she asks, "What is your name or nickname? What should I call you?"

The older man responds playfully. "Who do you think I am?"

The biblical reference causes Teresa to giggle and mischievously join in his banter. "I will call you, 'Teacher.'"

"Then, 'Teacher' it is!"

"I would love to hear more of your stories, Teacher."

He nods with mischievous delight. This bond between a charming woman and a wise older man marks the beginning of a beautiful friendship. Teresa is amazed at the wisdom and humor of this eccentric older man. Over time she grows quite fond of him and his muses. The knowledge of the dove, and the spirit of the Lord, have visited her once again. She is not entirely forsaken!

BE LIKE A CHILD

The next day, Teresa goes to the park earlier than usual in anticipation. She sits on the bench, waiting for the old man, now called "Teacher." Now it does not seem like such a terrible thing that Teresa's gray hair lines her roots. The example of an older adult indicates that growing old is nothing so fearsome. How has she warmed up to the teacher so quickly? Given her analytical mind, she tends to be cautious. It was bizarre and uncommon to connect with a stranger so spontaneously and immediately. He was like a vulnerable child with a charming heart, such an engaging quality, and he wears his feelings on his shirtsleeve. This gentleman makes her feel valuable—maybe because he listens well and without harsh judgments. He carries some mystery. Should she be more cautious? Quite the contrary, she is sure that her new friend has an integrity of heart and competency, like the friend she has often longed for as a spiritual advisor. At first, she directed animosity at this kind gentleman. How wrong she has been about the teacher. Now she loves his kind face. Two bluebirds start to sing to him as he approaches.

In his jovial fashion, the old man pauses and looks around before sitting, "Dear lady, would you mind sharing the bench with an old man?"

Teresa exclaims, "Of course not!"

"Are you sure?" The teacher teases as he sits on the bench with startled surprise and humor. He sports a look of great satisfaction. This manner of entrance tells her that things from yesterday have significantly changed, and she too is glad of the development and his mercy.

"So, is your friend still AWOL?" he asks. Teresa nods sadly. "Your lower lip comes out in a pout like a little girl when you become sad."

"Do I look childish?"

"In an adorable way."

Teresa gives him a questioning look, and the older man explains further. "It suggests honesty, not concealment, which is necessary for acquiring truth."

As Teresa understands, one must be honest first regarding their strengths and weaknesses to find God's kingdom. She addresses the teacher. "I am not a good fibber and do not want to practice that either. Furthermore, I expect others to be much more honest than they are, and I frequently find myself hurt due to my tendency toward trust or my style, as a psychologist, of looking at everyone's potential. I carry an over-sensitive trait. You know, Teacher, if I were to change, it would be a significant personality adjustment, and I would not be able to love so freely. I have tried to be less trusting, but I am not happy like that either, because you cannot accept and give gifts of love so easily. The person you trust must have your interest at heart and competence. I rely too much upon people's competency or sincerity of soul. I expect to meet Jesus instead of mere human beings. Even with Jesus, perfect trust is not easy. Doesn't that describe the path of a mystic? Ideal faith is not easy. Where we want to be is not where we are. Oh, how I would love that consistency, to trust and not be afraid! We must suffer to get there; it is extremely hard. However, as the ego decreases and God increases, one becomes more childlike and vulnerable. There is undoubtedly a cost to this way of being and such a great reward."

Teresa is now inspired to tell her own story about working with troubled teens.

TROUBLED TEENS

"When I began my career, I wanted to work with the most violent, troubled teenagers who had been through every type of treatment. They had been to every group home level and even to training schools for attempted murder, committed murders, and rape. They only let men work with such people, and the last therapist quit because these boys thrust a metal hanger through his back. I insisted, like a dog on a slipper, to be one of the first women to work with these troubled boys."

The older man growled as a dog would, encouraging Teresa to continue her story and making her laugh.

"I started with group therapy at the time. I walk into the room to see four white teenage males, sons of the KKK, and four black African American males. They are looking at each other with pure, unadulterated hatred. I put my hand up at eye level like this." She raises a hand, palm down, up to her eyes. "I say, 'Look, I will respect you if you respect me.' I approach each of the young men to ask their names. Each time I say the same thing. 'I will respect you if you respect me. Will you agree?' Each one agrees while finding the question puzzling and novel. The suggestion that they are worthy of respect is unexpected. They feel that I am dangerous or crazy. I expect them to behave like gentlemen; they are in my office. More bewilderment passes over their faces when they hear me address them as 'gentlemen.' It now appears that they are looking at the windows and doors for an escape. They think I am nuts. Eight juveniles, climbing all over each other in close quarters, make a mad dash to the door. As they do so, I reassure them. I am speaking to their potential. Weeks later, my supervisor asks what I have done to them because they usually enter the waiting room fighting and damaging furniture.

"One day, they want to test me and say, 'Ya know you should get your nose fixed!' They wait like they are expecting me to cry. So, I say, 'I don't want to get my nose fixed. I like to smell the coffee in the morning—in Brazil' Again, caught off guard, the whole room is full of laughter, and they do this together. That was the very beginning of the miracles of God."

The teacher smiles and tells her, "That is the virtue of courage: to work with those boys. Perfect trust is not easy. You encourage them to sin no more by looking at their potential. Where they want to be is not where they are. Oh, how you would love that consistency, yourself, to trust and not be afraid. People must suffer to get there. It is awfully hard. However, the suffering results in trusting and childish ways because the ego decreases, and he, your God, increases."

Teresa looks startled. "That can't be! To be trusting like a child is a weakness," she exclaims. She stops herself. "Wait! You are right. You are saying it is a virtue. The world tells us that it is a fault." He nods in agreement. "Oh, Teacher! That puts a whole new meaning to the saying, 'Unless you become like a child, you cannot enter the kingdom of God.' The world's opinions are often the opposite of the values in God's kingdom."

The older gentleman says, "Sometimes, God taps people on the shoulder to get them to look at things a separate way. Though uncomfortable at first, after a taste of the kingdom, they want more. I remember a priest's story about a tap from God."

"The purpose of my soul is to love God
The greatest gift is the freewill to do so
Which gives the reason for my very existence."

ALTIERO, 1998

Chapter Three

Thy Will Be Done

FATHER JOHN: HARDEN NOT YOUR HEARTS

One morning early in the day, a priest named Father John is preparing to leave the rectory. Father John checks his wallet for cab fare because it is an icy morning. Alas, from the look of things, he has just enough for the one-way ride. The obedient priest quickly accepts his fate and decides to walk very quickly to the church and ride a taxi back. He thinks to dress warmly and put on a thick, green, Irish sweater under his thin coat, which is all he can afford on a priest's allowance.

He adds his wool hat and sets off at a brisk pace, with the thought, "Walk fast; you will stay warm!" Father John is on the fast track, shuffling down the street and almost running. He remembers the days in college, just before his entrance into the seminary, when he ran track. It was a blissful time when he received his calling.

Father John's trip down memory lane is suddenly interrupted as he rounds a corner and hears a man's faint call, "Father John?!"

He is sure that it is a parishioner's voice, but he thinks: "Can't the person see that I'm in a hurry because it is freezing?" He has already run past the person; Father John cannot be sure that he has even heard his name called, for the voice beckons so softly. Nevertheless, Father John admits that he has heard it and cannot deny it to himself. Father John stops his jog and turns back to round the corner again. At that moment, he realizes that his wool cap is missing, causing a chill to his balding head.

He does not see a soul at first, but then he hears a voice say, "Father, why did you stop?" Father John looks down to find a young, homeless woman he does not know; she sits on the sidewalk wrapped in a tattered scarf. While still on the cold pavement, she dusts off his cap (which must have fallen to the ground). The young woman extends her hand, holding his hat (which she has retrieved) so that he can place it atop his head. "You dropped this, Father. You dropped your hat. It flew off your head—you ran so fast. I could not keep up if I tried." She is visibly pregnant and scared.

"Someone called my name, 'Father John!' Well, it was a man's voice." Father John looks around but sees no one. Father John asks, "Has he left?"

The young woman says, "No, Father, I said nothing, and no one is with me. I am all alone in this world. I do not know your name, but I prayed you would stop. I am all alone." Father John sees a frightened young woman, and now he is glad he has stopped.

"You are not alone!" He helps her up and flags down a cab to accompany her to the homeless shelter. Yes, he uses his fare money to send her safely to the Gabriel house for pregnant women. Mass starts late that day, and people wonder why Father John has tears in his eyes when he says, "If today you hear His voice, harden not your hearts."

After finishing the story, the teacher notices that Teresa's eyes are welling up with tears. He smiles. "So, Teresa, was Father John in the right place at the right time? Many people are passing by that morning talking on their cellphones, checking their watches, and do not notice the sad looks of a lost lamb. I have heard exciting stories about people being in the right place at the right time. When Father John left that morning, do you think his well-laid plan for the day was the essential plan? Have you ever found yourself running through life, only to be pushed off your direction by an unforeseen event? This event influences Father John and the young woman for decades."

COMPASSION AND GRACE

Having suppressed her tears, Teresa clears her irritated throat. She is as if burning with sadness. She recollects herself after the very heartwarming story. The priest has shown the value of conscious intention, compassion, and a disposition of flexibility to respond to an unexpected situation despite one's fixed plans or ego. A person may address given needs with compassion. Compassion prevails and alters the priest's clear course for the morning. This story contains teaching that encourages reflection about the will of God. How do we relinquish control with faith in divine providence? Thought, if truthful and honest before God, promotes growth.

After reflecting on the teacher's story, Teresa asks a question, expecting a humorous retort. "Is the girl related to the first homeless guy?"

Instead, the teacher's eyes rest upon her; in a sincere and compassionate tone, he states, "Dear child, we are all related." Both are silent for a long moment.

Afterward, Teresa deeply ponders the first two stories. By the time she arrives at the bench the next day, she has composed a dogmatic lecture; all prepared to impress the teacher who kindly listens. At the very end of her moralizing sermon, she states, "So, all those other people who don't believe in God are doomed to failure and will not achieve the graces we do!"

Teresa waits for agreement or even applause, and she is disappointed when the teacher asks, "Did we eat from the Tree of Knowledge for breakfast, little one?"

The truth of this statement stings. Teresa has made use of these beautiful stories for her ego trip. Out comes the lower lip and the pout that could soften a thousand hearts. She is afraid he will be so disgusted by her pride that he will walk away and stop telling stories. A tear flows to her cheek. Will he make an exceptional exception?

He wipes her tear with his finger and says with great love, "I think you will like this next one."

> "If not for his love it would have
> Been better to have never been born"
>
> ALTIERO, 1998

Chapter Four

Casting Stones

A PAIR OF WARM SOCKS

The homeless man's teeth stop chattering from the cold as he lies on his back and looks at the blue sky above him. He realizes, "I am in the last stage of hypothermia when a person is numb and feels no pain." The homeless man has a name, and it is Andrew. "If I were a religious man, I would be having a conversation with God right now, but I have been an atheist all the seventy-two years of my life." He turns his eyes to the right, toward his friend James, who is still shivering.

Andrew smiles to himself. His young friend will make it through the night—so long as he has something warm for his feet. Will this be the last time Andrew sees James? Due to his age and illness, the possibility of Andrew's survival through the night is doubtful. Andrew looks down at his own feet and his thick wool socks. "Thick wool socks for a dead man?" With his last ounce of strength and an earnest effort, Andrew removes his socks and puts them on his sleeping young friend. Shortly afterward, Andrew, who is an atheist, quietly passes away in his sleep.

Teresa's eyes are wide open in amazement as the teacher finishes his story.

ACTS OF CHARITY

"Is there virtue in Andrew's final act of love? What do you think is more important: what you think and believe, or your heart and the acts that flow from your intention?"

"Your heart, your charity, of course!" Teresa is placing her hand over her heart and, with conviction, proclaims, "Since Andrew is wrong and a loving God does exist, do you think Andrew's last act of courageous love will hold merit with this loving God? Some people will infer that a loving God would not abandon such a man since Andrew does not abandon his brother or leave him to die beside him while he sleeps. Other people may be just as certain that beliefs hold merit—while the absence of belief is a deficiency, as in Andrew's case—and their own righteous beliefs make them holy (supposedly). Some, though (like Andrew), may perform acts of love daily, regardless of their stated beliefs (or absence thereof). Do people judge as well as a loving God judges? There is an implied question here. I often wonder why people believe that they have the right to judge in such a way."

While the teacher nods his assent to her reflections, Teresa speaks tentatively and diffidently, aiming at wisdom this time, not pride. "Andrew is an example of a virtuous atheist. Those caught up in their moral values may exclude compassion. Without compassion, they may lack the hope needed to recognize the good in another person. The very righteous moralist, sadly, can be extremely far from love. This story creates space and structure to question our moral regimes and thinking routines and sort through and throw out all the rubbish we acquire from the Tree of Knowledge.

"To trust in someone's potential, even at the last minute of one's life, takes spiritual courage. Jesus shows this trust toward the repentant thief on the cross. What makes the repentant thief innocent? Not belief in the religion of the day nor even knowledge or recognition of Jesus as the Messiah. The thief admits he is guilty of a crime and that Jesus is innocent. Also, he has the faith and courage to ask Jesus if he may be with him in his kingdom. Spiritually, the thief becomes innocent (forgiven) when admitting his guilt.

"Unlike the repentant thief and Jesus, many use their moral compass to cause separation and to become an island unto themselves. Such a stance is often dogmatic, resulting in harsh judgments of other human beings. Jesus is met with harsh criticisms and accused of blasphemy by such opinionated people. Sadly, severe, and cruel aspersions, based on ideology, are internalized by people, especially toward marginalized groups, reinforcing their isolation from society. Laws and beliefs encourage condemnation today as they did during Jesus's day. Human beings are suffering from loneliness and pain rather than being approached with charity. Are isolated groups treated with charity? What if we all behaved like Andrew and saved suffering people from death or provided them with warmth from our resources?

"The group of teenage boys I mentioned earlier were so marginalized they could not comprehend that they deserved respect. A beautiful thing happened one day, which ended the isolation among the boys. The group's most feared teen was tall and muscular, and no one gave him a hard time.

When he was age six, his mother's death left him with his father's developing drinking problem.

"One day during group, I asked P.J. what it was like for him after his mother died. P.J. explained: 'He drank a lot, and I was scared because he was all I had. He would come home staggering through the door, vomit, and fall face down in it. I would tell him to come on and get up. Please, Dad! Get up! I didn't know if he was dead or alive, so I pulled him as good as I could to get him to the shower to rinse him off.' P.J. looked down at his feet. The entire room was silent. 'How old were you when this started, PJ?' I asked. 'I was seven; it got easier as I got stronger. I have done it every day—even now.' 'So, every day, you, a faithful son, dragged your father across the floor so that you could rinse the vomit off his face and restore his dignity. In your way, you were asking for love. 'Will you love me now? Dad, will you love me now?'

"P.J. began to cry a fountain of tears. As I looked around the room, all the boys were crying. Whatever the truth was, it resonated with them all. Could it be that all of humanity weeps with these boys, wondering if our heavenly Father loves us? Then I saw a most beautiful event. Each of the boys started to comfort him! 'P.J., you are a good son.' 'Man, I thought I had it bad; you were so brave at age seven!' 'P.J., we are here for you, brother; we are here for you!' 'I love you like a brother, man.'

"That day, those rough and tumble boys healed themselves and each other, and I got the honor of watching the beautiful potential in their souls. People should not be marginalized but approached with charity.

"Injustices can hurt any marginalized group, whether they are marginalized based on race, ethnicity, gender, sexual orientation, religion, age, and maturity, or just because they are different or belong to some other interest group or subculture. People can have differences of opinion. They need not turn these opinions into dogmas and sources of pride or use them with their egos to infringe on another person's free will or beliefs or practices—unless some violation of life is involved.

"Often peace and tolerance reside where healthy boundaries are permitted and established. By the end of my two years with these boys, they were having discussions like this: 'You know we are brothers! I love you, man.' 'Hey, if you are my brother, then why am I black and you are white?' 'That doesn't matter. I do not believe in my father's crap because he is full of hate. You can come over to the house.' 'I am not going do that.' 'How come?' 'Your dad will beat the crap out of you. I do not want to see you all beat up. Look, we will meet up as friends away from our home. Do not worry. It is all good.'

"Regarding the miracle of charity, the boys demonstrated benefits. The prognosis by professionals for these kids was that ninety percent would be in the state high rise, a maximum-security prison, within ten years. Ten years later, they were all married with children and contributing to society. The charity produced miracles.

"The idea that we can coexist with others, with varying views and opinions, is not promoted by society or the media. In a desperate search for meaning, some people establish a sense of belonging, yet without a moral compass, and acquire a sense of identity as members of an oppressed or hated (and hateful) group. Once these people establish themselves as victims, their actual emancipation becomes quite limited. They lose hope and can no longer be free; they are entrenched within a limited world rather than liberated by the truth and the word of God. We need to be looking for reasons to love, not to judge or hate. Love and its effects are frequently not found as valuable in this world."

Teresa winds down her passionate speech and takes a breath to pause from her excitement.

"Oh my! That was quite a bit in one breath!" The teacher's eyes are wide.

Teresa put her hands on her head as if squeezing it while whimpering, "I did it again? Too much of the Tree of Knowledge?"

"No, my dear student, that is wisdom because it is colored brilliantly—just as all these autumn leaves are golden—with great compassion."

Teresa feels as if she could dance on the fluffy clouds above her head. She gives her teacher a big hug.

VARIETIES OF CHARITY

As Teresa walks home from the park, she reflects on the stories they have exchanged. The old teacher must have a doctorate in philosophy or theology—from an Ivy League school, although he does not brag. All the characters in the stories are like friends and family. She loves them. How odd is that? There is great virtue in the people portrayed; for instance, the young girl brushes off the priest's hat, treating him like a brother, even though she has nothing. Are all these people individuals whom the teacher knows or has known? He must only know saints. Is she his first sinner? Oh no! She grows pensive for a moment. Would he someday tell a story about the pouting, arrogant, snotty girl in the park? The teacher is quick to forgive.

"It was as if he forgot my foibles as soon as I showed sincere compunction," she considers. "How strange. He prefers to look at my positive aspects, like my honesty expressed by a pouting lower lip. Jesus, wherever you are, thank you for sending this friend!"

The theme of sacrifice unites all the stories told by the teacher. Mr. Banks gives up his coat, the priest gives up his time and taxicab fare, and Andrew relinquishes his socks. Each takes the role of servitude or being a servant, disposing of themselves to meet the needs of others. In this way, people experience the joy of love. Jesus insists on washing the disciples' feet to exemplify the virtue of self-emptying for the sake of another's well-being. Thus, we may get a glimpse of divine love. Is that what Jesus means when he says, "Love one another as I have loved you"?

The degree of charity and its depth shows some qualitative differences. Mr. Banks has significant wealth; he gives comfort and reassurance to the homeless man. He may have renewed the homeless man's belief that there is compassion in the world. The priest has less material wealth than Mr. Banks but many more basic comforts than the lost young woman. The priest gives his taxi fare and attention with compassion. He does not want her to feel alone or abandoned. Chilled by her loneliness, his soul is more severely impacted than his body's chill while running in the cold to the church and back. He frees her from her loneliness and doubts about being cared for by humanity. Andrew has very little and gives all he has. Andrew sacrifices his life.

Teresa cannot help but appreciate Andrew especially. She is *sure* Jesus does: "This is my commandment, that you love one another as I have loved you. Greater love has no one than this that he lay down his life for his friends."

"Very few things in life are perfect
Those things of human origin cannot be so
However, a sincere act of mercy infused by the
Divine grace of God is perfect and the miracle of divine love."
ALTIERO, 1998

Chapter Five

Suffering as a Gift

"All suffering I endure is a gift of your mercy
So that I can learn to love and love again
to love, to love this is all and everything."

ALTIERO, 1998

Teresa sleeps well and awakens earlier than usual. So, she sits in her sunlit kitchen, sipping her freshly percolated coffee. She loves these special mornings when she can take time with her sips and listen to the birds chirp in the morning sun. The dew on the foliage glistens like pearls as they catch the luminous rays. For about four years, Teresa's sleep has been no more than three hours a night while taking care of her very ill husband. Before that, Teresa had spent nine months taking care of her terminally ill sister. Understandably, after an unusually restful sleep, she enjoys savoring the morning.

WHAT GOOD COMES OUT OF SUFFERING?

Each step of the way, during those difficult times, Jesus makes it clear that he is present, and Teresa remains in prayer while knowing that her dear husband will die. She asks Jesus for more time each time the doctors predict her husband will not make it. His life is extended by three years, much longer than the initial prognosis (just nine months). How can people stop praying in crisis? Prayer is her lifeline, keeping her from despair and giving her hope.

Due to his military service and asbestos exposure, cancer spreads from his lungs to his liver during the last days and then to his brains until he is blind. Letting go of love is heart-wrenching. He is suffering and waiting for her to allow him to go. Jesus tells her that it is time. The time is approaching. Through love, she will be resilient for her dear and courageous man.

Then, she says the most difficult words she can ever say, "You have been the joy of my life." He nods slowly. "That is not all. You made me stronger." He nods once more. "So, I want you to know, if you want to go—don't worry about me, I will be okay." He nods three or four times in goodbye, while a tear runs down his cheek, and he leaves with his last breath. Jesus has held her hand through the entire time.

Teresa has let go with love. She is stunned that she can do this courageously; even the home healthcare worker lets out a torrent of tears and hangs onto Teresa for comfort. This very young woman is inconsolable. Teresa is empty. There is no compassion remaining for herself or others since she has left the last drop with her husband.

THE WIDOW

A widow for one year, grief-stricken, joy flees from her life. Teresa continues to work as a clinician through everything. As a psychologist, she listens to the brokenhearted, attempting to use her suffering to connect with the grief of those who grieve, although they have no idea about her tragedies. Her suffering, it appears, provides a conduit for theirs. Oh, my goodness, has that suffering been a gift? A gift to humanity, in a small way? She changed after two miscarriages, for instance, and after her father's death due to Alzheimer's. Her suffering feeds love, which then nourishes many people.

Recently, a widow came to her office as a client. The woman sits in the office chair, close to the door, her eyes glisten with tears. The tears are faltering, afraid of falling, like the dew on morning leaves. She hugs her purse on her lap as if for some protection or security. The quiet woman looks at

Teresa with hesitancy. A single word or look could cause significant pain to this grieving widow. Every word Teresa remembers, every laugh echoing through the air by people walking by—just enjoying the day—can be harsh. Teresa has been there too. Will we never laugh again? The woman has put up a great fight through her husband's illness.

Teresa expresses insights into her pain that others cannot understand. The widow's well-intentioned family members make cutting comments like knives. Understandably, she isolates herself to avoid pain. Medication is not working. The death of this widow's husband takes numerous years of struggle with a terminal illness. She is exhausted and exhibits compassion fatigue. Tiny pearls of sorrow fall from her eyes. These priceless jewels cling to her cheeks one last time until they are on their way, like salty kisses from the ocean. Veils of confusion blow away, lifted gently from the brokenhearted.

God has given Teresa and others a great gift. Jesus turns pain into rejoicing. The eyes of the body may not detect the movement of love from one person to another. By the soul's vision, the gift of suffering is for the glory of God!

AT THE PARK: MEETING THE TEACHER AGAIN

In front of the big bay window, a woodpecker flies from a large tree to peck on the windowsill. The click, click of his beak alerts her that she may be forgetting something. The bird encourages her to come out of her thoughts and get to the park.

This morning the sky is slightly overcast, although there is no forecast of rain. A jaybird jumps on a branch above Teresa's head, dropping dew from the leaves onto her head. He is screaming at her as if she has made a severe park violation. Everyone knows that she is running late. She wipes the condensation off her head and says to the aggressive bird, "What is wrong with you?" To her chagrin, the comment ticks him off more, and he keeps jumping on the branch from one side to another, screeching loudly. "You are reckless and rude!" She scolds the arrogant avian. With that, he gives one last scream and flies off. "Jaybirds and mockingbirds are the gangs in the park, and everyone knows that!" she giggles. Teresa feels energized and ready for battle, this confidence she has not experienced for a very long time.

More golden leaves fall on the path to signal summer's end and the beginning of fall. How lovely they are, and how precious is God's grace on humankind.

That is the jaybird's issue; he does not want the season to end. Teresa finds the teacher, looking quite reflective, sitting on the bench. His dismay is out of character. She sits beside him in silence for quite a while. From his face, he seems to be reviewing the history of humankind.

There is much mystery to the teacher. How does she trust him so readily with all the unknowns? Usually, she is cautious, but she loses her caution with this old guy for some reason. He finally sighs and begins, "One of the most profound questions facing humankind is: Why is there suffering? One need only turn on the news for a few minutes to see violence, starvation, pestilence, war, poverty, natural disasters, and death. Sometimes, it is only physical death that silences suffering. People ask why there is physical death. They question why there is a terminal end to our physical existence. There might be no reason for it, some say. Others argue that a person is just a speck of dust floating upon a voice of uncertainty and diminishing into silence." A tear falls from the teacher's eye. "*They do not know how much they are loved.*"

What intense sorrow today. It is as if, upon the teacher's shoulders, he carries the world's suffering. The choice of topic for a story presents an uncanny coincidence given her thoughts earlier that morning.

The teacher continues, "If some people believe these notions, have they considered how the pain of such experiences relates to their quality of love and perfect trust? Are choices to love still available within all such incidents of suffering? Often to be courageous for the love and glory of God is humankind's legacy, revealed by the ability to survive and to spread goodness and compassion toward each other, regardless of the hardships or system of belief. If so, this legacy is a victory and singing to God's glory within heaven.

"My dear Teresa, if this is the case, then love has won. As many believe, if love has won and God is love, then God has won. If people embody the essential truth of trusting God regardless of circumstance, they will find less reason to be afraid and acquire perfect trust. The answer to human suffering is that the answer is in the question. If you are asking the *why* about individual events, then you have not achieved perfect trust in the will of God. Does great courage come from suffering? And incredible acts of love? Does love ever die? Is love eternal? Is God eternal?"

Teresa is silent in awe at this beautiful truth. Her husband's death is also fresh in her memory. The victory of love over death gives strength and wisdom to the soul. The teacher begins another story.

"Behold my sinfulness and weakness so that I may take comfort

In my dependency on you and desire to love you."

ALTIERO, 1998

Chapter Six

Mercy

THE GENTLEMAN AND THE JANITOR

Carl Wright is a confident man with strong feelings about a great many things. He is not timid when giving his opinion and does not hesitate to put people in their place. Carl is a man of great ideas, and the man sees many of his plans come to fruition, earning him great praise and accolades. He is eighty-five years old but does not look a day over seventy, so he is told by friends. Yes, Carl Wright is successful. He dresses the part and takes great pride in his accomplishments. Carl makes sure to affiliate only with those who meet his high standards. He avoids those failing to maintain appropriate vision and lofty stature.

Tonight, he is going to the opera with his wife and an impressive cadre of friends. The small, excited group departs from their limousine. Mr. Wright jumps from the car to impress his female companions when his foot hits a tangible object, a broom, which almost causes a frightening tumble onto the sidewalk. Obsequious friends cheer in approval of Mr. Wright's laudable balancing skill and attempt to conceal their fear of the man and his temper. Carl Wright holds onto his anger like a trapped bull when confronting the janitor sweeping the opera house's entryway.

Mr. Wright is furious with this senseless man and his broom, "My God! Don't you have anything better to do than to cause a patron a major accident with your broom?" Carl Wright dramatically adjusts his tie and checks the cuffs of his pristine shirt. He prepares to give the "ignorant" janitorial employee a piece of his mind.

He continues with his tirade until his party members become highly uncomfortable and say, "Oh come on, Carl, it is getting chilly! Why are we wasting time with the likes of him? He is just a janitor." Carl has just enough time for a final indignant look at the man, who responds with just a bowed head throughout Carl's rage. The women in the party giggle and continue with their joyful night. The janitor strolls to his second job at the nursing home, where he cleans; in return, the facility provides care, room, and board to his aging mother. He works very hard and loves others very much.

Days, months, and years pass for Carl until, one day, a tightness in his chest causes him to tumble forward during his midday tea. The butler knows at once that the master of the house requires medical care. Carl has a massive heart attack that sadly leaves him paralyzed. The general hospital transfers Carl to the local nursing home to recuperate. The nurses' aides change the sheets on his bed when they notice that he has also soiled his blanket. The nurses are tired and frustrated with the old man and say, "I guess you expect us to go all the way down to the first floor to get another blanket?" The man, due to paralysis, does not answer; he cannot answer. They know that he cannot speak but say, "Well, I guess you don't need one? Who is going to know, anyway?" The two nurses' aides giggle and leave.

Mr. Wright thinks they must be kidding. They will not leave a thin, older man shivering on his bed. Who could do such a thing? He is only wearing a nightshirt. Minutes pass: hours creep slowly by as he shivers through the night. Suddenly, he hears someone walking down the hall, whistling, and then he sees a broom. Carl thinks it is only the night janitor, but surely, he will take pity on the shivering older man! As the janitor is walking by the room, he sees Carl's curled-up figure, shivering but not moving and unable to help himself.

The janitor comes into the room and looks him right in the eyes. He recognizes Mr. Wright; everyone does. The odd thing is that Mr. Wright knows the janitor. He is the man whom he criticized in front of the opera house years ago. The janitor leaves the room with his broom.

"I doubt I will see him again. Why should I?" Carl Wright remembers what he once said to that man. Mr. Wright feels vulnerable for the first time in his life. He humiliated the man, pretending it was due to the man's ineptitude rather than admitting the truth: Carl's clumsiness was responsible for the fall. "How did that man feel when I gave him such a lashing?" For the first time in his life, Carl makes a silent plea to God, "Please forgive me!" And a single tear rolls down his cheek.

Suddenly, he hears whistling, and the janitor comes in with two thick warm blankets and quickly covers the frozen man. The two men's eyes met. Another tear rolls down Mr. Wright's cheek. Carl wants to say thank you, but he cannot move his lips. The janitor's eyes are full of compassion. Carl realizes, "This is a great man!"

"Don't you worry about a thing—I got your back, and I forgive you."

POWER AND VULNERABILITY

The teacher looks at Teresa. "Are you going to cry through all my stories?"

As her tears are streaming down her cheeks, she nods. "Yes, likely. I am an extremely sensitive person."

Teresa remembers the overcast sky, the screaming bird, and the last vestiges of spring upon entering the park how her mood has changed after receiving the wisdom of this older man, who is so honest and compassionate. He smiles as if he has hidden knowledge about her, making Teresa feel warm inside her heart.

"How did you expect the janitor to react, and why?"

"He reacts to Carl the same way you reacted toward me the first time we met in the park!"

"Come now; you weren't that bad!"

"Oh, yes, I was! You don't know what I was thinking."

"I don't?" The older man's tone suggests that he did know. "Do you believe that Carl's suffering causes a change in him? What might have contributed to the janitor's decision?"

"That kind, sweet janitor must have a history of great suffering and a giant heart."

The older man nods in agreement. "What contributes to the nursing aide's decision? How do the characters in this story fare? People often come to that fork in the road where they can be vindictive or show mercy. Those who lead with compassion feel better afterward. Teresa, it is interesting to consider how many opportunities people have, during their lifetime, for expressing love or hatred amidst their suffering."

Teresa processes this information, deeply and quietly, as she tends to do. "In this parable, we hear about Carl Wright, a noticeably confident man who has strong feelings about a great many things. There is also a janitor, a nameless man, quite humble and responsible. I notice there is no physical description of the two men. The chances are that people will entertain images of the two men representing various ethnic groups and races, according to their assumptions about life. Of course, the change in Carl suggests that both his suffering and the janitor's mercy profoundly affect him. He lets go of his tendency to marginalize certain groups of people. Now he is the humble recipient of another's kindness—just the kindness he has withheld from others.

"I wonder whether people hearing the story see some potential in Carl. Or do they see justice served? Are people moved toward sympathy and mercy? When Carl changes, some may think 'too little and too late.' If so, how receptive are they? And what is their disposition toward mercy and forgiveness?

"Another exciting theme of this story is that influential people and powerless servants exchange places. Those with power have control: the capacity to plan and act. Therefore, those with power (and gifts from God) have a moral responsibility and must be careful not to hurt vulnerable people."

As Teresa finishes, the teacher adds, "Yes, and the most vulnerable people would be the elderly and the unborn if one believes in a soul. In this story, people change roles. Although the janitor is defenseless at the beginning of the story, Carl is the vulnerable patient at the end. For this reason, we should serve each other."

"The message is: Serve each other as Jesus did by washing the feet of the disciples."

"Are you ready for another story?"

"Oh, yes!"

"Here's a story about a man named Tim."

Chapter Seven

Faith and Courage

TIM THE FIREMAN

As Tim waits, he hangs his head low and holds his hat in his hand. He wonders who the priest will be behind the closed door, who will hear his confession. Tim considered becoming a priest in college because of his love of God. However, Tim meets his beautiful wife, and what a distraction she is! Instead, he became a firefighter and had children and grandchildren.

He comments, "I am not saintly enough to be a priest anyway because I lack spiritual courage." Some of his brothers at the fire station could enter burning buildings without hesitation, but he always would pause. Doubt would flood his soul, but sometimes, a shove on the back from a fellow firefighter would get him to move forward, and he is thankful for that. This hesitation seems to be growing as he gets older. Whenever he hears of the death of firefighters, he remembers the loss of Jed. "God must know how I miss my best friend, Jed." Tears fill Tim's eyes now as he thinks of his friend, nicknamed Jed for Jedi warrior. Jed was always the first in the building and the last out. The day he died; he had ventured into the burning building to save a little boy's dog. Jed said, "I can't stand to see that little guy cry!"

Jed is a saint in heaven, something Tim believes he could never be. Tim knows what to confess; he is a spiritual coward. He decides to sit face to face with the priest rather than hide behind the screen, which is optional in the confessional. Upon opening the door to the confessional, Tim begins the ritual. "Bless me, Father, for I have sinned; it has been three months since my last confession." Tim looks down at his feet with great shame and reluctance to look at the priest; he tentatively relates his concerns.

After Tim's confession, he is surprised at Father Michael's response. "Tim, there is no sin in appreciating the life that God the Father has given you. There is no sin in loving your family, your wife, children, and

38

grandchildren. Tim, appreciating a friend and his virtue, well, that too is good practice." The priest's gaze is compassionate.

"But what if God wants me to do more someday and I freeze or fail him?"

"Tim, we are all simply human, feeble in our sinfulness, so at times of great difficulty, all we can do is ask the Lord, with humility, to give us spiritual grace to do his will." The priest's gentle kindness surprises Tim. Father Michael continues, "Tim, God is a merciful God, and he knows our weakness. For your penance, say one Our Father to help you to increase your faith and to know that it is okay to be dependent on God and to believe in his mercy."

A blanket of peace spreads over Tim that day, and the warmth of love embraces him. Tim is preparing for a great challenge that he will face later that day.

Father Michael smiles as Tim leaves the confessional. He is fond of Tim, and he has heard remarkable things about him from Jed during confessions before Jed's death. Father Michael considers all the New York firefighters that he knows who can indeed become saints long before he ever reaches such a state.

Though Tim is at peace afterward, he rarely goes to confession—perhaps because he is attached to his shortcomings. He loses sight of God's mercy and love. How wonderful God is! How incredible is divine love, much more wonderful and mysterious than our love. Tim's peace is so deep that the fire alarm does not disturb him. He calmly gathers his uniform and hat and jumps onto the fire truck. The truck's siren blares as it lunges toward the site, where a commercial plane has flown into a building, crashing against one of the Twin Towers.

Father Michael gathers his vestments. Many will need their last rites at the site where the devastation has taken place. A police car waits outside the church to take Father Michael to a hopeless place, where his light will guide the hearts of many and give faithful courage. Father Michael is shocked upon arrival by the scene. A second plane hit the top of a building. However, many are still stuck inside. The firefighters, who had arrived just moments before, paused for his blessing before they entered the building. Some of them look scared. Father Michael loves them instantly and, to comfort them, goes to the front of the line. He senses that God calls him to that position. Tim, who is putting on his helmet, looks up just in time to see Father Michael at the front of the line. "This is good, because I am following a saint into that building." Tim has no idea at the time that he, too, will become a saint that day.

As Father Michael considers the line of saints following him into the building, his heart fills with gratitude and a silent prayer. "Lord, fill us with your grace so that we can do what we must do. I offer our souls into your merciful hands." Then he begins to recite Psalm 23 aloud, "The Lord is my Shepherd; I shall not want. He makes me lie down in green pastures: He leads me beside still waters."

Tim hears Father Michael reciting his favorite psalm, so he too begins to pray aloud, "He restores my soul. He leads me in paths of righteousness for his name's sake." Tim again feels incredible peace and courage. As the men appear throughout the building, one saintly man comforts an injured person not to die alone. As Tim holds the hand of a tearful woman his daughter's age, the walls collapse around them.

Tim suddenly sees a smiling figure and gasps, "Jed, what are you doing here?"

Jed says, "I am so glad to see you!" He lifts Tim off his feet as if he were light as a feather. Tim is still assisting the tearful girl, looking with wonder at the two men because she is no longer afraid. Although looking back at where they have been lying, she feels a glorious peace; their bodies still appear to be there. Her injury is gone. Tim feels joy, not of this world, and he knows that everything will be okay. He sees a beautiful light emitting from the sky above Jed's head. Jed puts an arm around each of them and walks them slowly out of the building and into the clouds of heaven, saying, "Did you know dogs go to heaven? I found that kid's dog!" Sure enough, a dog sits at the celestial portal, eager to play.

The teacher turns to Teresa, who is crying again (as can be guessed). So, he hands her a handkerchief as a gesture of comfort. "Some people believe that when people die, the souls of the departed welcome them. They have great faith that God's house has many rooms. God prepares a room for each person to welcome them to heaven. People are at various stages of their journey. Nevertheless, there are always rooms in his inn. Can you tolerate the different paths and those times during the trip when you meet fellow travelers?"

Teresa speaks with contrition. "As you know, a while back, I became disgustingly arrogant regarding my values and how my beliefs must make me a better person. I proved that I am not a better person because I look down on others. Most troublesome is that my judgments keep me from charitable thoughts. I continue to feed my pride from the Tree of Knowledge. The deceitful one still offers those tasty apple morsels. I frequently gobble them up with enthusiasm. Yet now, I find it fascinating when courage and charity come forward during challenging times. I realize it is more important to understand than to judge a person. The priest exemplifies charity clearly when he speaks with the firefighter. The firefighter, who is quite lovable, gains courage by admitting his weakness and receiving grace in his sacrament."

Teresa adds thoughtfully, "You know, Jesus always led with love. For example, his conversation with the Samaritan women and with Matthew, the tax collector. They listen because they want that love. Even on the cross after great suffering, with great love, Jesus asks his heavenly Father to forgive his tormenters because they do not know what they do. He did that all the time. He took on suffering and endured with love. Hey, you know what? That is why I listen to you; it is love! Sadly, I think you must have significantly suffered then."

The teacher is touched by this and softly states, "Yes, Teresa, I love you very much. Tim brings his love to the injured woman because he has experienced the love of children and grandchildren fruitfully, in both good times and sufferings. So, when he looks upon this injured woman, his soul floods with compassion, and fear is absent. The heart flooded with compassion experiences significant pain; it is like pouring the ocean into a shell—it may burst! Where is there room for fear? Perfect trust is a union with God. The beauty of divine love is the wish he has for everyone. Divine love expands the heart, and it exudes this love. The soul burns with the blood of Christ, which leaves an inexpressible wound."

"There are only two things
For which I am certain
My sinfulness
And
His divine mercy
I have greater faith
In the second."
ALTIERO, 1998

Chapter Eight

Creationism

Teresa finds herself in less of a hurry the next day while walking toward the park. Nature's beauty that morning arrests her. The colors appear more vivid and the sky more glorious than the previous week. Are the birds excited as she is over the bursting flames of red decorating the fall leaves? Singing birds delight in the scent of the trees. The fragrance of sandalwood is now seeping out like tears of joy from the tree's sap.

Her friend's stories are profoundly changing her. Her mind is actively pondering questions for the advancement of her soul. What is the importance of experiencing love? What if life is a gift, a beautiful opportunity to learn about some great truth? So profound and yet beautifully simple, this truth can take more than a lifetime to learn because of its diminished value in the secular world. What if, through the soul's quiet perseverance and gentle call from an unknown source, it stumbles forward and trips for lack of humility, and then, just by grace, finds itself elevated at its level of consciousness and in love with the almighty God?

Teresa's heart is opening to a new way of being. She uncovers two levels of awareness, which are always present; many people no longer recognize one of these levels. Sometime after birth, when human memories form, perceptions are organized to make sense of our surroundings. Our human experiences overrun the soul's reality; the sensual pleasures are almost glorified if truth be told. Indeed, the human being finds itself with a bump on its head at birth such that it forgets its origins. The life of the senses pulls a person into activity, in the external world around them, to the point of idealizing the sensory realities (i.e., the sensorium). Whence we originate and emerge in time, the home becomes a lost memory; that other original place becomes a vague memory or only a dream.

The soul is in a panic. "When did I leave my father's house?" The soul yells into the darkness of the senses. The physical sensations restrict the person's capacity to sense with the soul and spiritually to see, hear, feel, touch, and taste. This situation is one of original sin, the cutting off from our divine origins. Alas, here, people deny their other existence, their natural home. Is that, OK? What harm can come from having eyes that cannot see, ears that cannot hear, hands that cannot feel the soul? The great mystics do not tell us that the soul's senses are quite different. The certainty of the soul's existence, and our connection to a vital source of love and mercy, go way beyond the limitations of our temporal being existence. Why haven't they informed us? Or if they have done so, is it possible that we do not hear?

"The way to love is gratitude to God

My love and my all

Your precious love

Your divine mercy

Your infinite wisdom

You my God have

Broken my heart."

ALTIERO, 1998

Chapter Nine

The Eyes and Ears of the Soul

Teresa finally reaches the bench. The teacher is not disappointed by her slight delay. Instead, he is engaging the monarch butterfly that has landed on the upper side of his cane. On a perch of sorts, the butterfly sits on the hoop and entertains the teacher with a beautiful ballet. The teacher, with a joyful expression, is gesturing and smiling to share the moment with Teresa. He holds his hand over the tiny creature as if he is a puppeteer fluctuating his fingers. The butterfly flaps her wings under his suggestion. Eventually, he points to the sky and releases the imaginary strings. In response, again acquiring free will, the butterfly takes flight but first taps the teacher's nose in farewell.

Amazed, Teresa asks, "Did I miss any other miracles this morning?"

"You know, all of life is a miracle, but the greatest miracle is faith, because with faith, you can recognize all the miracles!" He takes the time to notice the birds flying above their heads in synchronicity, and Teresa follows his gaze. The birds are euphoric. "Teresa, I believe that you are ready to hear some stories about events seen with the eyes and heard with the ears of the soul." The teacher speaks wisely like a sage.

"How strange, I was thinking on my walk to the park, how my life has changed. I may have entered the dark night of the soul. However, a strange flame illuminates the night, giving me hope and faith, even though I am standing in the darkness. I hunger for God, but I trust in him. Why then am I so hungry? I remember feeling this hunger in the night as a doctoral student when we had to visit the prison system."

"The dark night happens to many and in diverse ways. Even among the hopeless like the thief on the cross. What happened that day, Teresa?"

"I saw Jesus conquer hell. It happened through prayer. A light in the darkness, which banished that deep pain of the soul—for I was a prisoner to the pain I witnessed. During our doctoral fieldwork, we visited inmates within the prison system. Shall I tell you the story?"

"Please."

BREAKING OUT OF THE SOUL'S PRISON

At the prison, the first institution is minimum security, and inmates walk about quite freely, for they do not have a strong history of violence and aggression. They appear pretty content; their confinement is only temporary. Then there is the medium-security prison and then maximum. Each state of detention is more daunting as the security increases and the demeanor of the inmates' changes. The prisoners that are "lifers" are disgruntled; they have nowhere to go, and, surprisingly, they taunt the males (more than the females) with catcalls, grunts, and lascivious innuendo.

The next place to visit is the most dreaded: death row. The male students are scared; because the lifers have given them such a tough time, they expect that the next group will be even more aggressive and that, in the small quarters of death row, there will not be as much distance between the inmates and the people. I am afraid of all the hopelessness there. The guard explains that the inmates will be facing the wall of their cells, a standard of behavior required to avoid mishaps. The guards say they do not always do it on purpose, but sometimes, they lose control and urinate on the floor. The urinary incontinence may happen out of desperation and the knowledge of their impending death.

The guard announces, "Under no circumstance will you speak to the inmates!" We entered the small dark area. A silence fills the room, very still, and the only sound is the minor hum of a fan, with a purposeless, mechanical sound coming from the back of the death row area—what a hopeless void, a bleak existence. The backs of prisoners face the people, their shoulders hunched in resignation, their heads hung low, and their eyes cast down onto the floor. They look less like people and more like souls resigned to their insignificance; they appear lifeless in humanity, like the morbid wallpaper on the back wall of their cells. The students enter hell to view the souls in cells, sustaining their lives in darkness, tediously filling the empty void of their existence—my intuition charges fueled by compassion. My eyes leave the cells of the prisoners. All I can do is silently hang my head and pray in desperation, "Why am I here?"

There is a man, with shoulders sorrowfully drooping, his frailty expressing resignation, the spirit of a man facing a dismal fate, who is calling out from soul sorrow. Simultaneously, I am closing my eyes once more, and misery is flooding my heart. Why is this man here? Then the voice of my soul is loud and thunders, "Look, look at him. Look at him now!" With great pain, apprehension, and tears welling up in my eyes, I look up as compassion rips through my heart. It hurts, and I speak aloud to the man in front of me. "Would you like me to pray for you?" There is an audible gasp from the other students as they wait for a reprimand from the guard. Watching the man, I do not fear the guard, my heart breaks under the weight of God's love and sorrow for the man.

The convict is startled by the question. Who would pray for him after what he has done? He raises his head slightly, and his soul responds to this gesture of merciful love as he gently nods in agreement. I begin the Lord's Prayer aloud, again causing a cautious reaction from my fellow visitors; their eyes quickly check with the guard. The words of the prayer fill the cell with hope as seen by the soul's eyes and light; yes, the light is beautiful. When finished, I look up to see the prisoner, a child of God. He nods twice in gratitude as a tear runs down his cheek.

The teacher holds Teresa's hand, absorbed by the story. He adds to it. "Before the student visits, on the previous night, following his final meal, a soul despairing has asked God for food for his soul. Tearfully aware of being undeserving, the hopeless man has implored God to grant him the favor of beholding love before departing from this world. 'God, I know I am undeserving, but if you are here, show me by a final act of kindness so that I can believe that you forgive me for the unpardonable.' God has sent his message. Though humans punish, God is merciful and often makes the exceptional exception."

Tears are glistening in Teresa's eyes. Her tears are now part of their everyday ritual. Just as customary as their smiles. She and the teacher shrug; by now, they expect tears from meaningful stories.

"Teresa, this is an excellent story! In this story, where do you see hope? Where do you see faith?"

"Quite often, hope follows humility. Humility follows acts of faith. There is a relinquishing of control and total dependence on God."

The older man nods in agreement. "How might the eyes and ears of the soul be different from the senses of the body? What is the food for the soul?"

Teresa furrows her brow with intensity and then responds tentatively. "Teacher, the soul's vehicles for seeing and hearing are hope and faith. Food for the soul is the grace and truth that come from God, granted in response to our asking. Hope and humility are present for the prisoner—for me, faith and sorrow."

"How does fear sometimes keep us from reaching out to others, and what does spiritual courage mean?"

"God gives graces, maybe humility, to obtain the virtue of spiritual courage. Both the prisoner and I pray, with modesty, and exercise our free will to ask for God's graces. I have heard that humility is the cardinal virtue of Christ; there is something to that belief or truth. God's mercy is different from human compassion, vaster and wider than all the sky, and more plenteous than the stars in heaven above; God's patience displays extraordinary fortitude. God's strength is bigger than all the oceans and seas. So, there are no words to describe the infinite attributes of our almighty God! We should ask more often. He delights when his children ask."

The teacher grins as if quite pleased. "Yes, the truth is humble and simple. It leads people to glorify God." The teacher looks up toward the heavens as if in silent prayer. Teresa follows his gaze. They sit in silence. Peace quiets her soul.

After what seems like an eternal moment, the teacher turns to Teresa. "That was a nice moment in contemplation, wasn't it?" Teresa just nods because she is still trying to understand the peace that has overcome her. The teacher smiles at her. "It is interesting how you can talk less and less and listen more and more when you have abandoned the Tree of Knowledge. All that planning people do, and they miss the big picture."

The teacher taps his cane and begins his next story. "I knew a young lady whose father tried to encourage her to hear through the ears of her soul. Her name was Isabella."

"I am just a speck of dust,

floating upon a voice of uncertainty,

and diminishing into silence,

yet he has not abandoned me.

My hero, my strength, and my love."

ALTIERO, 1998

Chapter Ten

Reflections of God's Love

ISABELLA AND HER FATHER

Patience has always been tricky for Isabella. She stands on the stairs of her stoop, shielding her eyes from the sun, slamming her foot down, and muttering under her breath, "Where is he? Where is he? Where is he?" Now, she begins an incessant tapping with her left foot as if that will speed things along.

Her father, John, is perplexed by his beautiful daughter's impatience and compulsion over timeliness and punctuality. He has become a tired older man but has not lost his sense of humor. John chuckles while thinking, "Why are the young in so much hurry? It is not as if they were running out of time as we are, and I have slowed down."

Isabella hears her father's soft laugh, which warms her heart as it always has since she was a little girl. He has been peering at her through the tiny window of his row house. Her behavior is amusing to him. He wanders outside to extend their visit. Isabella adores her father. Both he and her mother have made great sacrifices to send her to school. They had never left their tiny brick house, her birthplace, and they could have had so much more, but they sacrificed it all. Isabelle has planned to make it up to them in time, but then her mother passes away, unexpectedly, in her sleep one night while Isabella is at school. This unexpected event breaks Isabella's heart, and she vows that she will be courageous for her father, as her mother would have wished her to be.

Her father, John, wobbles onto the porch with his cane, pausing as he gazes at his daughter. She is the perfect likeness to her mother. He smiles again. It would have been awful if she had looked like her father. An old goat is not a fitting model for a daughter who happens to be his little princess. Isabella is watching her father engage in one of those conversations in his head, for he tilts his head to the right, with a questioning expression, and then to the left with a nod as he finds a suitable answer.

Often, while he considers many options without saying a word, Isabella teases him relentlessly. "Hey, what's going on in there? Anybody home? Who is winning the argument?"

Then one day at school, her friend Peter says, "Hey, penny for your thoughts? You are doing that thing that your dad does."

Isabella denies it. "I am not doing that thing!" It tickles her to know, though, that she is a chip off the old block, for she secretly admires her father's analytical ability and believes that he is among the wisest men in all the world.

Her father's kind words have pulled her through the hardship of losing her mother. In confiding that she has wanted to make things up to them, he simply responds, "Dear child, love is a choice." Isabella looks puzzled. So, he continues. "Love is of more value than anything in creation. Love is the essence of our souls and the reason for our being. To love you as we have had been the greatest joy of our lives. How could you give us more?"

This response makes Isabella cry because he says it with sincerity and joy. He rocks her in his arms as she weeps, and he can comfort her like his little girl, something he has missed since she has grown up.

Isabella's father feels a twinge of guilt as he recalls that he has lied to her the previous week about having to walk with a cane. "Oh, it's that darn arthritis. It's gone to my knee." Two weeks before her visit, he had suffered a mild heart attack, which left him with a bum left leg.

Her father likes Peter, Isabella's friend, whom she later marries. Peter is a good man who loves Isabella. John hopes his daughter will not be annoyed with her future husband, though; as everyone knows, punctuality is not Peter's forte. "I am sure he is fine, just a flat tire at most," John says. Isabella feels comforted by her father's words.

He appears even psychic at times. However, when she asks him how he knows things, he claims that God talks to him through his heart and soul.

"Do you hear him?"

"Yes, but not the way you think, not with my ear."

"Good thing! Because you are one deaf old man."

Her father laughs up a storm. "Well, I heard that."

Now on a more serious note. "Pop, did God tell you that?"

"About Peter?" He smiles and nods. He speaks slowly, weighing each word. "You know, Isabella, I do not have to be the go-between between you and God because I am not much more destined for this world. When you hear the voice of God, listen, child. He calls you with the sweetness of a loving father. He brings you peace and comfort not found in this world of things that appeal to the baseness of the senses. Learn to listen, child; just listen!"

Finally, Isabella sees a familiar car approaching the house. As she turns to let her father know, her father begins to topple forwards, driving his clenched fist to his chest.

"Dad!" The sound of terror in her screaming voice sends Peter running from his car. John instinctively knows that it is his time to talk to God and make peace with those he loves. Isabella's father offers a gentle smile at his daughter as he investigates the face of love. John will not die alone. Fortunately, Peter is late. If he had come on time, both Peter and Isabella would have left the house, and John would have been alone. So, instead, her father dies by looking into the face of love, the greatest treasure of his life.

FATHER LOVE

The teacher proffers the following questions. "How many times have your determination and impatience proved less influential than an unexpected event? If a person stops trying to control every moment of every day, they are more likely to be mindful of the present moment. When faced with a choice, John's option to love is a priority and appears so easy for him, leading to the question, why is that?"

The teacher turns to Teresa and finds her in tears. He kindly strokes the top of her head with his hand. "There, there, little lamb. You have lost your father?" Teresa tilts her head slightly and nods yes as her lower lip quivers.

Teresa's relationship with her father has been tumultuous due to her father's tremendous financial stress. He is responsible for five children and his wife. He is often suicidal. Teresa, at the age of twelve, is appointed by her mother to discourage his suicide. Teresa's mother explains that if her father dies, the children will reside in foster care because she does not even have a high school diploma and cannot get a decent job. Teresa becomes exceptionally good at talking people down from suicide. She never has a single suicide on her case load as a therapist. She attributes that to all her practice with family members and divine providence.

Sometimes her father's temper is severe. One day, during her childhood, Teresa begins to cry as her father is slapping her sister. Out of nowhere, his mighty fist strikes Teresa in the face, sending her flying. He is wearing a ring that leaves her with a black eye, swollen jaw, and busted lip. The two girls run to safety in the bathroom and lock the door. After things settle, their mother tells Teresa that she would have to lie if asked at school how this happened. She says, "Teresa, if you speak of this, you and your siblings will be put in foster care and will suffer molestation!!" The following day, Teresa's father calls Teresa to look at her face, and he cries. He cannot believe he has done such a thing. Teresa is afraid he will kill himself. She can feel his turmoil; she has that gift. "It's okay, Dad. It does not even hurt. I bruise easily." The pain in her father's face is unlike anything she ever witnesses again.

Oddly, the experience strengthens her, preparing her for her future calling to work with the most violent teenagers in her state. Her father never gets over that incident. She is always trying to help him to stop hating himself. One day decades later, she says to her father, "You know, Dad, I think anyone who has more than two kids goes straight to heaven."

Her father's eyes widened. "You think so?"

"They are saints, all of them. So, Dad, will you advocate for me to Jesus someday?" Her father nods. However, what happens next is unexpected.

"Would you like to know what I am going to say?" She nods, thinking that it will be quick. He begins slowly, "My Jesus, I would like to tell you about my daughter Teresa. She has a truly kind heart. I know you have seen that she has dedicated herself to your lost and suffering people. She works with the poor and the neediest people, feral children with severe mental illness. She sent herself through school. She has served the children of God because she has a great love for you." Her father continues speaking for thirty minutes before he turns to his daughter and says, "How is that?"

Teresa is crying an ocean of tears. Her father somehow has given back to her what he believes he has taken away from his daughter so long ago.

The teacher is looking at Teresa now with great compassion. "He knows you love him greatly and love never dies. In the story about Isabella, John evinces love of the kind that your earthly father has for you and still does. Your earthly father gives you a glimpse of the great love your heavenly father has for you. Love is eternal and abundant."

Teresa leans on the older man's shoulder and weeps for an exceptionally long time until the ballet dancer butterfly returns and taps her on the nose. She giggles and notices the older man's expression. "The sun is setting, my dear; a chill will arrive soon. So let us bid our farewells so that we can meet again tomorrow." Teresa gets up to walk home slowly, very slowly, and she takes the time to look up at the night sky and the sparkling stars. She greets them most lovingly, "Hi, dads!"

"A miracle is only as great as the faith behind it.

The greatest miracle is faith."

ALTIERO, 1998

Chapter Eleven

The Mystery of Forgiveness

Mike and his wife are entering the park, and he is wondering if the unusual woman will be there today. The sky is a canvas of light blue, and the fluffy white clouds form mountains of whipped cream in the heavens. Both he and his wife have acquired the healthy habit of walking in the park before work. He thinks it is suitable for his health and his marriage. The night before, when Teresa is having a private conversation while leaving the park, Maggie, and Mike drive by in time to notice Teresa talking to the stars.

"She is leaving the park rather late," Mike says.

"Yes, the park closes but don't worry. People unusually do not bother people who talk to themselves," Maggie retorts.

"Doesn't that make her more vulnerable?"

"No, just more unpredictable, which may mean dangerous to those up to no good. Maybe we can talk to the mysterious woman someday."

Mike laughs. "So, we take walks to get away from curious children, but then we become the curious children in the park?"

"Point well taken!"

"Maggie, I could have sworn I saw her talking to that old guy we saw on the bench once."

Maggie rolls her eyes. "I know, Mike, you told me at the time, but there was no one sitting with her at all." Maggie decides he needs a new prescription for his glasses. "When was the last time you had your eyes checked so that a tree does not look like a person?"

"Point taken." He knows what he saw; he just wants to avoid an argument.

Teresa feels an unusual calm today, as if a story is unfolding right in front of her. All the stories open issues from within and make things clear and straightforward.

Teresa notices a burst of red leaves, a vibrant flame covering a tree. How beautiful fall can be. Upon drawing closer to the tree, a startled red cardinal flutters to his feet near her nose.

"Oh, I am so sorry! I didn't see you hidden among these red leaves." He is not too distraught and looks at her with a bit of curiosity, tilting his head from one side to the other. The friendly bird meanders away a couple of inches as if allowing her space to sit on the branch with him.

Teresa laughs. "Oh, believe me, you don't want me to join you on that small branch, dear one. Are you moving over as the teacher did? Oh my gosh, how long have I been with this bird? I better hurry!"

Teresa hurries down the path until the top of the teacher's grey head appears. She slows down. The teacher is not restless—it seems that time does not exist for him. Whatever the reason, Teresa is glad.

"Hello, teacher! Are you having a lovely day?"

"Any day with you is a wonderful day!"

She plops down beside him. "Well, it appears that you have become quite a charmer."

"Yes, I can be at that."

"Unfortunately, not all relationships go as splendid as ours, teacher, and I wonder why?"

"Teresa, what do you think causes problems between people?"

"I guess misunderstandings, for one, and hurt feelings."

"Yes, indeed, but what makes people lack a resolution?"

Teresa furrows her eyebrows. "Hmm, they are stubborn or too proud? Well, sometimes they have just been hurt. I do not know. Some things are just too hard to forgive."

Teresa has herself been angry enough to kill someone—long ago. She has almost done so. At the age of ten, she passes by her elementary school on her way to her best friend's house, four blocks away, in an upper-middle-class neighborhood. The neighborhood scarcely has any crime at all. After passing the school, she comes to a small patch of woods with a bridge, which goes over a creek with metal bars on both sides. A group of about five boys, aged fourteen, are exploring around the bridge and waterway below. It is common for teenagers in the woods to build forts, smoke cigarettes, or just joke around.

One boy is balancing on the bars of the bridge. He has a strange smirk on his face, which Teresa does not recognize, making her uncomfortable. She is about to pass by the strange boy when this awful guy suddenly pulls out a knife and puts it to her throat. She stops immediately. He snickers. "I want you to come and do something with me." He is unequivocally suggesting something sexual. For some reason, unlike a typical ten-year-old female, Teresa is not scared.

Her pride swells as the insult settles upon her defiant, angry personhood, which is stunned by his stupidity. It does not matter that he is four years older; he is ten years stupider, and she decides he will die today. Teresa has the highest IQ in her elementary school, and she has been reading about fulcrums the day before. She recalls that the effectiveness of the lever depends on the position of the fulcrum. That would be his sorry butt. So, as he holds her wrist, he rocks back and forth, gathering energy and momentum; he assumes that she will fearfully pull him in toward herself, get her wrist back, and bring him to a standing position. The boy does not consider that by flinging her wrist toward him, he will spiral backward.

The prospect of an arrogant dimwit hurling through space is delightful to the ten-year-old, who gives no further review of her plan. The idea is comical and worth a good laugh. The snickering moron will be terrified as he rocks cheerfully. Welcome him to his death! Without further study of her particular flavor of vengeance, undoubtedly that of a hot tamale, Teresa flings her arm toward him. As expected, his sneering, confident smile vanishes. In its place, there is a startled look of terror as he falls backward off the bridge.

The boys scream like a castrato of choristers. Fortunately for the victim, before he reaches rock bottom, another boy comes out from under the bridge and breaks his fall. The male choristers sing in unison, screeching, "You could have killed him!"

Now satisfied with their horror and the feeling that she has total control, she states glibly, "That was my intention." The boys all gasp, looking at her like she is a monster, bewildered whether she may be possessed or merely mad as a bat. Teresa pauses to sneer at their frozen, shocked faces. She turns her back and slowly walks away, fearless, and victorious, at least for a while. As the years go on, the guilt torments her because she realizes she could have killed him.

Nevertheless, when she tells others the story, they are happy with her victory. Why isn't she? First, the boy has been the monster. Then she becomes the monster. How can she change this?

FORGIVENESS

Teresa finally snaps out of her walk down memory lane and says to the teacher, "Honestly, I cannot comprehend how Jesus did it. Well, he is a sacred person. He suffered greatly. How can he expect us to do it so well?"

The teacher nods with each comment to let her know he is listening but appears to wince when she mentions how Jesus suffered. Nevertheless, he finds the point that Teresa is conflicted about. "How does one forgive? Questions related to forgiveness and mercy are tough to answer because people have difficulty forgiving. Understanding mercy is complex because humankind experiences significant catastrophes, numerous wars, threats of destruction, and broken hearts due to multiple losses. One thing is for sure: One cannot make someone forgive by telling them to ignore the violation. Often, forgiveness arises due to our significant discomfort as we hold on to resentments.

"The fodder for these resentments is judgment as to what should or should not be in a just world. One's perceptions of another's intention and judgments increase a person's suffering. These demons are from the world of 'ought,' which drives people beyond the golden mean into intense emotions and extreme positions. People make themselves sick. Those who choose the less-traveled path to forgiveness, however, report strange experiences. They may disclose relief or an unburdening as if a weight is lifting from their shoulders. They become genuinely free.

"So, you might wonder how someone gets there. Where is the map? A qualitative difference exists between the people who forgive and the people who want to ignore the violation because they think that is the right thing. They often believe they can take the fast track and make the decision to dismiss what happened. However, not everything is black and white. People cannot turn off their emotions like water from a faucet.

"Through life lessons, people learn where their path lies and how to walk out of darkness or despair onto the jewel-cobbled path of forgiveness. Once they find this beautiful treasure, they often wonder why they have not seen it before. So, it is odd how life works! I want to tell you one of my favorite stories now."

"I am all ears!" Teresa exclaims gleefully.

"I want to be your little lamb
For all eternity."
Altiero, 1998

Chapter Twelve

Divine Providence in Forgiveness

COMPASSION IN UNITY

Jacob is glad that the summit is over. He is looking forward to returning home to Israel, although it will be a long journey. He is one of the first to board the plane and hopes there will be a bit of room to stretch out. As the attendant informs him, however, it is expected to be a full flight. As a rabbi, Jacob leaves behind multiple responsibilities. The death of loved ones aggrieves many grieving families. Jacob has recently lost his brother, who stood for peace and mercy until he was killed the previous year by a bomb from an adversary. Jacob's heart has grown hardened. Enough of those Arab fanatics!

People are now beginning to enter the plane much more rapidly. So, Jacob looks up to see who is entering his row. A man comes up, pleasantly smiling, with a cross dangling from his necks. "A rabbi and a minister," he says, "This flight should be interesting!"

Jacob nods to the man as he considers his remark. What a ludicrous statement! That man believes that Jesus is the Messiah, but he is merely a rabbi. How interesting can that be? Why do so many of the ministers he meets remind him of car salespeople? Jacob does not like sitting by the window. He asks the foolish, smiling man, "Would you prefer the window seat? I do not enjoy heights, nor do I enjoy looking out the window."

The minister replies, "That would be great. I love the window." The men nod and exchange seats.

That is when it happens. A man enters the plane, and Jacob's face turns to stone. The minister is surprised to see such an angry look from a rabbi. So, he follows Jacob's gaze to the man entering the plane. He is carrying his cap and a Qur'an. He pushes his glasses further up on his nose, having finished his midday prayer. He is an imam.

The minister thinks, "Oh Lord, I hope he is not a terrorist."

The imam sees the rabbi, and his nostrils flare. He recalls trying to counsel his neighbor as his child died in a bombing. In turn, Jacob is traumatized by the terror that has seized his people. The imam pauses and takes the last seat next to the rabbi. The Christian minister thinks this seating arrangement could not have been planned any worse. So, he avoids an international incident by looking out the window. They are all quiet for a long while. However, they each have many ideas and conceptions about the different characters in their midst: Christians (nosey, overbearing, and ethnocentric), Jews (greedy, rigid, demanding), and Muslims (hate-filled terrorists).

Then it all begins with the voice of a child. "But mummy, I dropped my car, and it is under his seat! I cannot reach it."

The Christian man thinks, "Oh my! Please, lady, do not even try! Get the kid under control." The imam thinks, "You'd better get your car quick, kid! That Jew will take it." The Jewish man (Jacob) looks under his seat and sees that the toy is under the imam's chair. So finally, Jacob makes a snide statement audibly, "Well, young man, it appears that your car is under the seat of someone who is not willing to budge or share his area with a child." This snarky comment is all that is needed to start the argument.

The imam retorts, "Me? Problem sharing? You arrogant—!"

The minister immediately tries to take control of the situation with a tone of authority. "I am sure that if we all just—"

Abruptly, the other two men cut him off in unison. "Mind your own business!"

The rabbi continues, "What is it with you Americans? You're always butting your nose into other people's business."

Then the imam pipes up, "Don't you respect boundaries?"

"Me?" the minister wails, "You guys have been fighting for years with your stupid bombs."

Suddenly, a hushed silence falls over the plane. Has someone said "bomb" on an airplane? The little child pipes up, "Mummy, what's a bomb?" The flight attendant approaches all three men with a stern, maternal look, and her arms on her hips. She says, "Really? Really?" Suddenly, the plane shudders, coinciding with an announcement throughout the plane: "Please stay seated within the upright position and fasten your seat belts." The flight attendant glares at the three men. She takes her seat to buckle up.

The pilot's voice, sounding a bit nervous, announces, "You must remain seated. We will be making an emergency landing to check one of our two engines, which has malfunctioned because of a sorry flock of birds."

The minister, looking out of his window, sees a massive storm approaching. The pilot has not mentioned the shower. The rabbi catches the minister's distressed look and leans forward to gaze out of the window. The clouds look ominous, and lightning is already visible. He leans back in his seat. He does not like windows on airplanes. The imam leans forward to look too. There's thunder, and a sandstorm forming below, which the other two men had not noticed. The imam begins to pray silently, as do the rabbi and the minister.

It all happens so suddenly. The shuddering plane takes a violent dive, and the oxygen masks drop down abruptly. Nobody can remember the breathing devices because the plane suddenly becomes dark before the crash. Jacob's strenuous breathing awakens him; he is wheezing because of pain. A rib is fractured or broken, but his leg has the most significant problem. He is afraid to look around, and he asks himself, "What is that horrid smell of something burning?" Now his memory slowly returns because of his throbbing headache.

"I was on a plane," he realizes, "It must have crashed. That smell must be burning bodies. I am in that Christian hell that I have heard of." The rabbi Jacob winces in pain. He is afraid to look around, but he knows that he must do so because of the possibility of other survivors.

Jacob gently turns his head to the left. He does not like what he sees. He weeps at the sight of a tiny hand clasping a small car. Jacob has not cried for an exceedingly long time, but the child's innocence touches him within the deep recess of his heart. His murdered brother, while standing up for peace, was recently killed. His brother, concerned with children—like this child—who are suffering deeply because of all the bombing. Has Jacob forgotten what his dear brother stood for? Love may replace hate, and peace can abolish war.

There is a great deal of smoke. Gray billows of clouds engulf Jacob, making it hard to breathe. Jacob hears a sound, a step of a foot or that of burning rubble. Wait, there it is again, and closer now. A soot-covered man is emerging from the smoke like a dragon, towering over him. "Rabbi, did you make it here too?" The ash-covered man is holding his arm as if broken. There's a cross still dangling from his neck. It must be the minister to welcome him to the Christian hell, of course.

Nevertheless, Jacob is delighted to see him. "Please call me Jacob, and what is your name?"

The minister winces as he uses his single arm to sit by his new friend. The cross continues to dangle as he holds his injury with the functional arm. "David. My name is David."

Jacob is startled and blurts out, "That was my brother's name!" David soon sees the little boy and begins to weep, and he cannot pull himself together. Jacob taps David's hand. "I felt the same and did the same. It is all right if we have compassionate hearts." David's soot-covered face shows the path that the tears have traveled right down to his neck. Something about this man's temperament reminds Jacob of discussions with his younger brother, David. David's persistence, "I don't see why you don't understand that peace is not possible through revenge and violence. Children are dying!"

"You are too idealistic! What is wrong with you?" Jacob would retort. His brother's face would have a pained expression as he turned abruptly, departing and shaking his head in futility.

The following morning David did not meet Jacob for his usual brotherly cup of coffee. Jacob enjoys coffee with his brother and feels disappointed. After waiting an extra twenty minutes, he took his coffee alone. Jacob said to himself, "Oh, revenge is not the answer, but is it okay to treat your older brother that way if he is giving you sound advice as an older brother should?" On the promenade, where they usually walk after coffee, the birds were pecking on the path because it was about time for David to throw those crumbs of bread.

Up the path, a figure was waving at him with a wide grin. Children encircled him. Jacob chuckled. He was not angry at me. The children run off giggling and laughing. David was walking toward his brother but stopped to pick up trash, an empty box, hoping for bread crumbs for demanding birds. David had a puzzled look; his horrified scream echoed throughout the promenade, "Jacob, stay back!"

An explosion, a thunderous roar, sent them flying backward. Another person's body broke his fall. After the explosion, he could not hear a thing. There were clouds of dust and smoke while people were running back and forth, with silent screams painted on their faces. Why couldn't Jacob hear their voices? His head and ears throbbed. One man tried to pick him off the floor and appeared to be mouthing: "Bomb, bomb!" One of David's friends was now running toward Jacob, weeping. Jacob read the man's lips. "David, your brother, is dead. It was a bomb. We must get out of here. You need help."

Jacob closes his eyes while listening to the voice from long ago. "We have to get you out of here. You need help!" Suddenly, it was not the voice of his brother's friend. The sound is no longer the voice from the past, but the sound is present, the living voice of minister David. His brother David died in a bombing. He is gone, and Jacob did not have the chance to speak to him, to tell him that his older brother had been just a stupid man who loved him. The minister David, in the present, taps Jacob's hand to bring him back to the current reality. "We have to get you out of here. You need help!"

After some time, they assess their injuries. Jacob has a broken leg and fractured rib, but he can walk with a splint. However, David cannot put Jacob's leg in a splint because David has a broken arm. David will not leave

Jacob. No, he will not do it, no matter how many times Jacob pleads, "Save yourself! You are irrational." Jacob is getting upset; this fool will die for him, and he is too idealistic. Jacob is about to protest when he suddenly realizes that he used to accuse his brother David of the same thing the day before he died. His brother David, like this minister David, was just too idealistic. His brother was younger, and Jacob was giving him advice and direction.

Suddenly, Jacob becomes quiet. He was wrong in his remarks about his brother, as being too idealistic. "I was controlling, just as I accused this minister of being," he reflects.

A person is now stumbling forward, from about ten feet away, toward David and Jacob. Someone else has survived. The person moves forward like a blind man with hands extended, shuffling a few feet at a time, stumbling as if his foot has hit a rock. The man cannot see well. David speaks up, "Hey! Are you drunk, or are you blind?"

"I cannot see from far. I have lost my glasses. No, I am not drunk. I am Muslim, and we do not drink." David reaches out his functioning arm to help the man sit down. They are in the presence of the imam. The imam leans forward to see David's face, "Oh, it is you." Then, he leans forward to observe Jacob on the ground and affirms, "Oh, it's you too!"

David says, "I am David."

Jacob states, "And I am Jacob."

"I am Muhammed." The imam crawls to the other side of Jacob to identify the slight blur behind him. Muhammed begins to wail. Muhammed is rocking a boy in his arms. He remembers rocking his friend's son a year before after the boy succumbed to mortar fire. Both Jacob and David try to comfort Muhammed but to no avail. Then abruptly, Muhammed stops rocking, his eyes widen, and he swings back his fingers to the little boy's neck. "I think I feel a faint pulse!"

David and Jacob yell, "Are you sure?"

Muhammed says, "Shh! I am a doctor."

Both Jacob and David inhale but do not dare to exhale so that the good doctor can hear. Muhammed is correct. He reaches into the boy's mouth, pulls out a wad of bubble gum, and begins to breathe into his mouth.

David notices that Muhammed may have slightly dislodged the gum with all that rocking. Jacob thinks, "This doctor is terrific!" They wait and wait. Then the little guy coughs.

What a sight it is, indeed! All three men are joyously happy. David and Muhammed jump up and yell. They begin to dance together like fools, and poor Jacob tries to sit up to join in the joy when the pain in his leg calls all of them back to reality. The little boy is startled and disoriented for just a few minutes, and he then realizes that something is very wrong. He has no mother any longer, and, as one would expect, he weeps for quite a while. Muhammed, Jacob, and David take turns consoling the child, each man recognizing and appreciating the other's compassion.

As the little boy weeps, they all realize the harsh reality. Jacob reaches out and puts his palm on the little boy's cheek. Muhammed continues to cradle the tiny survivor within his arms. David nods, adding comforting words, like a father to a beloved son. After these consolations, when the last whimper of sorrow leaves the rosebud lips, the men nod in silent agreement. Nothing in the entire world is more critical right now than this little boy.

They are all united, connected directly, joined as a single human family. Out of their sorrow comes laudable strength; endless spiritual might spring forth upon their foundation of love. The rabbi, the imam, and the minister will get this precious child back to safety.

David asks, "What is your name, son?"

The boy responds softly under his breath. "My name is Peter. Mother calls me, 'Peter, the rock.' She told me that I am trustworthy and brave."

All three men nod, and Jacob states, "You are brave, Peter! You are brave and strong, indeed." Both David and Muhammed gesture in agreement. Jacob tries to sit up again but winces in pain. "We need to get young Peter to safety. Please leave me and get him to safety."

"We will not leave without you." David retorts. David assesses the damage: his broken arm, Jacob's leg needing a splint, and Muhammed's limited vision. He shakes his head from side to side to match the hopelessness he feels.

Peter looks at the three men with childlike innocence and faith, "This is funny. Muhammed is a doctor, but he will need David's eyes to fix Jacobs's leg. Muhammed and David will have to help Jacob walk. David and Jacob will have to help Muhammed see." Then little Peter adds with chagrin, "But what do I do?"

All three men laugh in amazement. "Little Peter, strong and courageous, you just keep coming up with great ideas." The three men quickly go to work as Peter, their mascot, observes their actions. Soon all three men and one boy are stumbling and dragging each other north to Saar in the small country of Bahrain, eventually arriving at the American Mission Hospital, a satellite clinic in Saar.

The three men never lose touch with each other again. They all watch Peter grow up to become a wonderful young man working in international relations. Over the decades, the three men became a band of brothers, often eliciting surprised looks from those who observe their unusual friendship given their various backgrounds.

For the first time, after one of the teacher's stories, Teresa is smiling. Forgiveness puts a smile on people's faces. The older man smiles, too, pointing an index finger up. "Well, isn't that something? The three men change from being miserable to joyously happy. Something changes in these men because of their experience. Consider how suffering often brings people toward forgiveness. A child's innocence similarly impacts these three men."

"Teacher, fear plays a prominent role in our inability to forgive. When I forgive, love has trumped fear and given me the courage to do so. However, sometimes it is so hard to find love amidst animosity and anger. I understand why Saint Peter wanted to cut off the soldier's ear. If I had been in the garden of Gethsemane, I would say, 'No, Peter, it goes like this,' and I would cut off both ears. Peter might tell me, 'Teresa, you are a bad influence!'"

This honest and humorous story makes the older man laugh. "Teresa, when has forgiving someone been difficult for you?"

Teresa searches her mind but can only find partial truths. It is certainly easier to forgive someone you like or love. So, seeing the good in another person is the first step, but not always. "I can forgive if I see that another's motivations and intentions are not to cause pain; however, sometimes they do have harmful motivations. There is no simple answer to this question, at least in human terms. A sacred truth usually reveals the big picture. It is difficult to forgive when you are angry, afraid, or hurt by someone without redeeming qualities. I lose sight of the big picture. The difficulty may go beyond the other person and me. I may turn inward, and I forget the importance of perfect trust. I forget that divine wisdom flows like a stream through even the most horrendous suffering, which is allowed for a provident purpose. When I cannot forgive, I do not see this good purpose. Is it because I do not want to?" Teresa appears anxious and at a loss in response to when forgiving someone has been difficult.

"Divine providence and perfect trust unite the souls of the suffering. Whenever we have a common goal due to suffering, there may be some resolution. Jacob, David, and Muhammed find a common goal: they have faith and hope to protect innocence. Peter's life represents for them the human family compassionately. With this new vision, they break down walls of division, which brings divine providence into reality and lifts their souls with the courage to accomplish this goal."

OPENING THE HEART

Teresa remains unsettled. "I feel like I am in a dark room swiping at cobwebs and afraid that I may find a black widow spider. I get to a mirror. I do not like what I see: anger and hate. I do not want to become a monster!" Suddenly Teresa catches a glimmer of truth in the mirror. "I understand. Someone hurt my husband as a child. I found out two weeks before he died. What this person did is ghastly, and the person did it repeatedly when he was so young and innocent. It ripped up his insides. After a related surgery, ten years into the marriage, the injuries left him unable to be intimate; he was afraid his wife would leave him, so he did not tell her about his abuse. The doctor told her someone had hurt her husband but thought it best if the husband spoke to her about it. Initially, her husband denied it all, but two weeks before he died, he admitted that the terrible thing had happened numerous times."

Pain and anguish pass over Teresa's face. The teacher notices that Teresa is speaking in the third person, referring to herself as the "wife" of this husband, though she does not see how she uses this style to distance herself from pain.

"Most attributes have positive and negative aspects," the teacher says. "Your passion manifests in the many good things you do for people because you care. Great passion is often the source of charitable works. The evil one does not like that, so he is relentless in taking your attention away from charity work and diverting it toward hatred and anger. Teresa, you are trying to manage this problem with your intellect, not your heart. You are talking in the third person as if observing rather than being. Trust your heart and the love you hold inside. You could have left your husband as he feared, but you did not, and that enraged the evil one. You did not give up on love, and you gave your husband an excellent example of what love is regardless of the depravity in his family. The devil wants you to think you did not rescue him, but you did with your love. He left this world in peace, and you were his light in the darkness."

Teresa gestures agreement as she cries some well-overdue tears. She softens as she recalls memories of the love she and her husband have shared. They were best friends and spent most of their lives in intimacy and laughter. Through divine providence, a common goal is to look at the good that can come from a terrible situation. Teresa has done that most of her life. She can learn to forgive even more. Often forgiveness needs to be directed toward oneself. Sometimes people take too much responsibility for the pain of others they love. It gives the illusion of control and that they can control such events in the future. Hatred ensues in a feeble attempt to obtain reassurance about the future. Again, a lie within a lie is presenting to interfere with healing. She cannot change what happened to her loved one. Has she forgotten how much God has loved her? The evil one would be happy with that.

Teresa remembers the boy on the bridge who hurt her. It would be best to pray for him because he is likely a father now, and he would pray for her too. An eagle passes by. Teresa feels better having reconciled with herself. In the mirror in that dark room, tears are visible, streaming down her face, and Teresa tells her reflection: "You don't look like a monster to me." Through the ears of her soul, she hears the evil one howling in pain.

Finally, Teresa says, "I love that story about the minister, rabbi, and Iman! I am glad that their road to forgiveness took them away from their suffering by putting love first."

The teacher nods and says, "It often does."

"Is that Jesus's secret: Put love first?"

The older man laughs. "Dear Teresa. It is no secret! Are you ready for another humorous story? What does it feel like when someone forgives you?"

"See love, look for love."

ALTIERO, 1998

Chapter Thirteen

God's Comforting Bird Poop!

As a teenager, Jill is in one of her moods. She watches her mother sweep the patio with the determination of a woman on an earnest mission. Her mother seems obsessed with her task, which prevents her from appreciating the clear blue sky above her head. Even more infuriating to Jill is that her mother ignores her presence, so she taps her foot in an irritable state. How silly my mother is with all her cleaning. In Jill's mind, her mother is cleaning all the time. What is it with her? Jill states, "Mom, put down the broom! You are always cleaning."

"You could help me."

"And what? Have a bent over back like an old woman—like you?"

The woman pauses and rests on the broom handle to respond patiently to a petulant daughter. "I have a lot of work to do."

"You always have work to do, and most of the time, you make it up all in your head. You're a cleaning fanatic." Jill's mocking agitates her mother.

Putting her broom in one hand, Jill's mother points a crooked finger in her daughter's direction. "The problem with you, young lady, is that you think you are perfect."

Ready for an argument, Jill pauses a moment with a defiant glance in her mother's direction. Her mother expects her to back down and contritely admit that she is not perfect. Jill will show her. She will say something unexpected; then surely, she will win the argument. Jill gives her mother a victorious glance and a wicked smile as she states boldly, "I am perfect!"

Not missing a beat, a large bird flies over Jill's head and simultaneously, as she speaks, plops down a large glop of white poop on her long dark hair. I cannot begin to tell you how devastating that disaster can be for a vain princess of Jill's variety. However, as soon as she screams, with a desperate sound of a teenage girl in distress (it sounds like the screech of a car), her mother is right on it. Jill's mother dutifully takes her spoiled brat of a daughter into the house toward the sink. She puts Jill's hair under the faucet. This experienced mother does not hesitate to put her fingers into the poop, getting her hands dirty while rinsing it off and attempting to calm her hysterical daughter. Her daughter's attitude toward her, moments before the bird poop fiasco, is of no concern. Forgetting the belligerent daughter, Jill's mother can only see her child, on the verge of tears, who needs her help.

Jill is in tears, not because of the bird poop in her hair. Instead, Jill feels great shame. She has treated her mother so poorly and has gotten what she deserves. Why didn't mother gloat? If in that position, she would have reveled in this minor disaster. Instead, Jill's mother responds with love as a mother who forgives her daughter's impertinence, displaying the humility of servitude.

Suddenly, Jill realizes the presence of God in heaven. God has caught her during that moment of being out of control. God has sent a loving and humorous message to let Jill know that she is way too impressed with herself. Again, she feels shame, alongside an awareness, and dawning gratitude, that God has taken care of her by sending a gentle message that she is way out of line—with her brash manner. Jill then says, "Thanks, Mom, and I am sorry. Here I am, acting like a big jerk! Why did you still take care of me and put your little fingers in my poopy hair?"

Jill's mother crosses her arms over her chest and takes a step back as if looking at her daughter for the first time. "That is a mother's love." Jill cannot recall a day or time when she had respected and loved her mother more than during that day when humility triumphed. Her mother's servitude is impressive and reminds her of Jesus as he washes the disciples' feet before his death. The deceitful find comfort in the lies of the world, but the graceful sheep find comfort in humility when suffering.

The older man looks thoughtfully at Teresa. "Some people want to win the argument at all costs. Jill's mother exhibits the kindness of God. She displays mercy like God's mercy with Saint Paul when his sight is restored even after persecuting so many Christians. He asked for forgiveness with sincerity of heart.

"Teacher, I think Jill did, too. The humility of Jill's mother is striking. It is a funny story but also sweet. Jill's arrogance turns into an appreciation of both her mother and God. She feels his love and is aware of divine providence. God reprimands her, letting her know he is watching. His watchful eyes are perfect. His love comforts her."

The teacher smiles. "Tomorrow, I would like you to tell me some stories, about faith or perfect trust, which complements our discussion of forgiveness quite well. Can you do that?"

Teresa is shocked by this unexpected invitation. After a rest, Teresa will be ready. For the love of the teacher and God. "OK. But don't expect miracles!"

The teacher laughs. "My dear, the sun will set soon. Will I see you tomorrow?"

Teresa looks startled, "Of course. You bet!" she gushes.

The two excellent friends then take their leave.

Chapter Fourteen

Faith

This morning, Teresa is in a delightful mood, walking briskly, humming a tune as she waves at the curious couple passing by in their car. The sun is out, the cardinals are singing, and the fall leaves are floating from the trees, spiraling down until the ground quiets their spin. Teresa is glad that her stories quickly come to mind. The teacher did not say that the information must be fictional. However, if she tells him that the accounts are accurate and true to her own life and that she is the main character, it might be embarrassing. So, she decides that she will change the main character's name to "Rose." Then she can avoid humiliating herself, disappointing the teacher, or just looking like a horrible person. She can break the story into three parts just in case he expects many fables.

A little squirrel is watching her as he munches on an acorn. There is an odd human being approaching, who is having conversations inside her head. The behavior leaves the squirrel a bit wary since he cannot guess whether Teresa regards him as prey, as if she is a predator.

"Good morning, Mr. Squirrel. Are you having an enjoyable day?"

The squirrel's eyes widen in alarm. A person talking to a squirrel is not right in the head. Simultaneously, grasping the leftovers of his acorn, the cautious animal flies up a tree; it is a perfect position for dropping pieces of shell onto the top of Teresa's head as she passes by. Teresa decides the squirrel is a bit of an introvert until she feels bits of shell on her head.

"Hey, cut it out!" she cries.

Mr. Squirrel lifts his tail as he scampers further up the tree out of harm's way. The pussy willows are in bloom, quite lush and fluffy. The soft fluff of the clouds of the earth is like lamb's wool. Teresa continues her walk toward her favorite bench. The teacher is leaning forward on his cane with a smile of welcome. Teresa sits by the teacher, looking askance, lifting her eyebrows, and tilting her chin in his direction. He smiles to himself and nods; yes, he will give her something to consider on the topic.

"A person once said that if people only had enough faith, they would see miracles all around them." The teacher extends his hand to emphasize the glory of the burgeoning beauty of the park. "The greatest miracle of all is faith. Again, suppose you have faith, the courage of perfect trust, then all of life is a miracle—although some ask whether it is a fool's folly, faith is a courageous act committed when facing uncertainty. A soldier once told me that courage is not the absence of fear but the presence of action when one is afraid. He said that war frightens everyone unless they are insane. That statement made a lot of sense."

The teacher lifts both hands as if offering a gift. "Faith as a concept gives many people reason to pause and reassess their place in this world and creation. Hope and doubt are predecessors to belief and despair. With heroic effort, people wish their faith to exist. The Apostle Thomas desired to have faith. The desire came from witnessing the joy and peace in his brothers. He pleaded with the other apostles to help him. Others persist in their disbelief and mock a fascination with mystery as a waste of time, the mere passing of time for idle hands and minds."

Silently, the teacher waits to hear Teresa's views.

Teresa nods thoughtfully before responding. "It is what it is, and most people attempt to discern their place within the universe by living their lives. Various dogmas and religious tenets sometimes create a separation between people. Some people who believe certain things believe that they are better than the people who do not think in the same way. The profession of opinionated dogma is the realm of people who claim to have faith and people who do not have faith. The devil runs the world through comforting lies, and we find the truth in the humility of suffering."

"Teacher, how amusing it is to assess both sets of people, who believe that they have all the answers regarding the universe. Here we sit with our finite minds trying to make sense of the infinite—what a ludicrous effort, Teacher! What if none of us has the answer? Is that all right? We could find a common goal in which to place our hope. We could agree that compassion and kindness, directed toward every human life, is a good reason enough to preserve humankind. Can we agree on a love for humanity? People may claim that we cannot agree, given our history of wars and hatred of one other—and all out of ignorance. However, the faithful suggest there is still a reason to hope and love because humanity has survived, and there are some laudable achievements in peace. We are still here, and we have endured quite a bit together."

The teacher smiles and whispers, "Blessed are the peacemakers. The Sermon on the Mount is a favorite teaching in the Bible, Teresa. Now let us explore the mystery of hope and faith through the eyes of a finite soul: you. Your stories, Teresa!"

Teresa takes a deep breath and begins her tale. "This one is about learning from others."

Chapter Fifteen

A Calling from God

Rose is an impatient and aggravating teenage girl. One morning, her mother, Nancy, reaches her limits regarding her daughter's demands for answers. Her daughter makes inappropriate demands directed toward God, and now, she is certainly going over the top. In her mother's eyes, Rose is disrespectful toward God by saying, "Father in heaven, if you do not tell me what that dream is about, or what I am supposed to do about it, I am just going to say it was a regular old dream and nothing more."

Rose is at her wit's end. She has never had such vivid dreams before, and she strongly feels her recent experiences come from God. The dream leaves her with joy, not of this world. Nothing on earth could make her feel such a delightful ecstasy again. It could be that God wants her to become a nun. Rose frowns at the idea, for she likes boys too much. Though God is authentic in her life and more than trustworthy—very real—Rose is fearful because she simultaneously wants to run and hide and to please God. What a mess!

God is asking her to do something but not telling her what. Why would he do this? Again, Rose starts her demands aloud, "Father in heaven, if you do not tell me what that dream is about, or what I am supposed to do about it, I am just going to say it was a regular old dream and nothing more. I am expecting an answer today!"

Rose's mother's eyes bulge in terror, "Rose Serrano. That is blasphemy! You cannot talk to God that way. That is a sin!"

Rose thinks for a moment about her mother's angry words. "I do not believe it is a sin because it is a cry for my Father's help in heaven. He knows that I am terrified and a bit rash. We have many discussions about that." Rose considers her mother's words and, in desperation, begins her final pleading. One drawn-out word arises with a groan from her mouth: "Please!"

Her mother, Nancy, conscientious about the time, zips closed Rose's suitcase and places it by her daughter. Rose is off to visit her cousin at Villanova . She does not know why but she wants to go. Soon enough, Rose's mother is pacing at the train station because Nancy does not see the conductor. How can she inform him that her young daughter is traveling alone? What if her daughter does not know where her stop is and the destination station, where she must get off? The train conductor finally walks by to the front of the line, where they are standing. Nancy calls out, "Mr. Conductor, could you please tell my daughter where to get off? She is so . . ."

The conductor continues walking forward. He does not hear Nancy because he is yelling, "Last call, all aboard!"

Nancy is exceptionally distraught now. A woman says, "I can tell your daughter where she can get off." The offer is coming from a person standing behind Rose. Nancy is so stunned that her lips appear to move without emitting sound. She cannot say a thing. Standing right behind her daughter is a nun in her full habit. Rose is turning around; she is not surprised at all. She is simply happy and relieved that God has understood and sent her a messenger about her dream. Rose smiles at the nun.

The nun bends over to talk with her. "You have something to discuss with me, don't you?"

Though Nancy is left speechless, her daughter responds joyfully, taking the question in stride. "Yes, I do, and I am so glad that you are here!"

Teresa now smiles at the teacher's posture. He has his right elbow perched on his right knee, with his hand under his chin, suggesting total interest. Teresa is very relieved that she is not boring him yet. "I have some questions for discussion as you always do. But we can discuss them when I am through. For example, what are the remarkable differences you see between mother and daughter in this situation? They both have something to offer, but they also lack in other areas. Rose is rash but trusts in her heavenly father. Her mother is patient and respectful, but she may need more courage to trust in God. Have you experienced a strange coincidence like this one, or have you heard of such before?"

The teacher says eagerly. "This is an excellent beginning. Now, go on with the rest of it!" Teresa smiles with delight; this is going well, and she continues.

Chapter Sixteen

A Nun's Friendship

Rose gladly sits down with the nun, who explains that she is the Mother
Superior from an abbey in Pennsylvania and a chemistry teacher. Rose loves
her instantly; she thinks something special about her, for her eyes sparkle
like the stars with a gentle delight and love.

Mother Superior says, "Now, my dear, what is it that you need to talk
to me about?"

Rose bites her bottom lip and whispers, "A dream."

The nun nods for Rose to continue. Mother Superior notices that Rose
is hesitating. "It appears that you are now having trouble talking about it.
Would you like me to start with my dream first?"

"Oh! Yes, Mother Superior, please!"

Mother Superior begins her story like this: "I once had a dream that
I was on my knees praying in a church. Suddenly, the doors from the back
of the church open. For some reason, I know that it is my Lord." Mother
Superior is overcome with emotion and begins to shiver. "He is carrying a

statue of his Sacred Heart, and he is coming to give it to someone. I hope, 'Oh, let it be me!' But then, thinking myself too proud, I say, 'Oh, if it is the Lord's will, let it be me,' and I cannot help it. I want it to be me. My Lord reaches me and pauses. I think, 'Oh, let it be me!'"

At this point, Rose observes that Mother Superior's entire body is shaking with emotion. Rose holds her breath as Mother Superior continues. "Then the Lord begins to walk again past me, and I am so sad!" Mother Superior's disappointment is quite visible. Her shoulders are slumping, her head hangs low, and her eyes close sorrowfully.

Oh no, how sad for this dear nun.

Then Mother Superior begins again. "I am so sad, but then I whisper, 'Not my will, Lord Jesus, but let thy will be!'" A huge smile crosses Mother Superior's face, and she says, "Suddenly, my Lord backs up, turns to me, and hands me the statue. I have never been so happy in my entire life. Now, I am Mother Superior of Sacred Heart Church in Pennsylvania."

Although Rose feels joyful for Mother Superior, she is aghast at the thought that she might have to become a nun, for she likes boys way too much. Rose exclaims, "Mother, that is a wonderful story, but I do not want to become a nun. I like boys too much."

For some reason, this comment makes Mother Superior laugh, and with love, she says, "Are you ready to tell me your story now, dear child?"

"Yes," Rose admits.

Teresa is pausing and looking at the teacher to see if he has lost interest yet. He seems delighted, to her relief. She muses, "If I were to ask questions, I would say, why do you think Rose is afraid to tell her story? It appears that Rose is comfortable with disclosing her story only after Mother Superior tells her story first. Why might that be? Have you ever been in a situation where someone else opens up, making it easier for you to do the same?"

The older man, tilting his head from right to left while considering her thoughtful question, does not respond because he knows it is not the end of the story and that Teresa has more to tell.

"Although I do have some questions for discussion, I think that what has happened between the two of us already provides answers to the previous questions. So, I will tell one more part. You have made this easy." Teresa continues her story.

Chapter Seventeen

What to Do with a Gift from God?

ROSE'S DREAM

Now it is Rose's turn to tell her story to the nun. "Well, Mother, it is kind of strange. Do you know how normally, when you dream, you know who you are? In this dream, I am not me. I do not even remember my name. I am standing near a well during ancient times, and I hold a basket of folded linens on my head as a shield from the sun, I believe. I must get to my daily business with the laundry when a group of women comes running toward me. We know each other quite well. We all dress as Hebrew women do during that time.

"Some carry baskets as I do, and some do not. They say, 'You. You are there! The one with all the questions. You always have those questions that we cannot answer. Now, the teacher is here. He is speaking in the desert. He can answer all your questions. You must come!' Although the demands are annoying, I am also quite curious. I explain to them that I have too much to do, but one woman grabs my arm and pulls me toward them. I do not remember when I put the basket down or why I finally go because of the woman's urging.

"I do not remember walking too far. There is a crowd of people sitting on the sand in a half-circle, listening intently to a man standing in front of them, not standing straight up with pride but bent to lean toward the crowd. The woman leaves, saying, 'There is your teacher.' I march further. My soul is stirring just by his appearance and the intent looks of the audience. I think, 'This is certainly a great teacher,' but then a gentle voice comes out of no-where, correcting me in a whisper, 'This is the greatest teacher of all time.'

"The sound of the voice is not odd. The voice of the Spirit is familiar from an early childhood experience that I vaguely recall. The voice is comforting. I go further, and when I arrive behind the teacher, I fall to my knees.

An overwhelming feeling entraps me that I cannot explain. It is impossible to put into words other than to say that a great love emanates from this man. It is an honor to be in his presence. I want to touch him to get his attention because his back is facing me, and my soul is yearning, desperately begging for him to look upon me. If I can touch his sleeve, but then the gentle guidance of that voice returns. 'You are not worthy to touch his sleeve.' I listen to the message, I know it is true, but my heart is yearning, 'Oh, Great Teacher, just one look, one look, that is all I ask.' All I can do is put my hope in him. Then, to my surprise, the beautiful teacher is slowly turning to face me."

By this time, Mother Superior's eyes are welling up with tears, and her face glows with the faith of a saint. Rose is shaking, for she is in tears herself. "Then, Mother, I see his beautiful, beautiful face. The face of unconditional love, and I fill up with this love. Nothing else in all the world or heaven is needed. This face, his face, oh, beautiful face! The voice comes again. 'This is the face of a man who loves you so much that he would die for you.' Suddenly, I am overcome with a desperate desire to thank him. I try to fall prostrate on the ground to express my gratitude. Instead, my soul lifts from my body, soaring far above the clouds. Joy, not of this world!"

Teresa must stop herself because of her intense emotions. The teacher notices that Teresa is crying. He gently nods in encouragement, and Teresa continues.

Rose says, "So, you see, Mother, I woke up greatly saddened knowing nothing of this world will ever bring me such joy again. Oh, this was Jesus. I close my eyes all the time, trying to see that face again, to have that feeling, but I cannot, and I do not. My heart is hurting. I carry a wound from love. What does he want me to do? I am afraid that whatever it is, I will not be able to do it because I am frequently so weak, rash, and stubborn. Oh, Mother, what does this dream mean?"

CONCEALED AND OPEN MEANINGS

Teresa takes time to blow her nose. Then she poses the following questions to the teacher. "Have you ever had a dream which is a communication from God? Have you ever had a dream that spills over into your waking life like the one Rose had? If Rose told you that the story was true, would you believe it? Why or why not?"

The teacher smiles. "Oh, but I do believe it, my darling girl. What did Mother Superior say?" The teacher has seen right through Teresa's use of the name Rose to conceal her identity.

"Well, Mother Superior says the following to Rose."

Chapter Eighteen

The Parable

Mother Superior is listening intently to Rose's story with a look of gentle peace and love. She does not interrupt, but her gaze is uncommon; it is as though she has one foot in this world and another in a distant kingdom. Nevertheless, despite this dual presence, she answers Rose's question directly. "It means that someday you will do something in the social sciences, and you will help a great many people."

Rose is startled for two reasons: first, Mother Superior's countenance shows certitude, and second, she suggests that the assignment is significant.

"You mean a social worker?"

"No."

"Do you mean a psychologist?"

"Yes." Rose is astonished by the dear nun's certitude. "I have a parable to share with you," the nun continues. "There is a chemistry teacher and an exceptional student. Oh, how the student loves the teacher. The student frequently looks up at the teacher with such great love that the teacher thinks, 'This is certainly a special child.' The student so loves the teacher that, to be helpful, the student stays after class. The student tries to help and often pushes a cart that holds vials and test tubes to the back of the room to store in the closet. However, the student is often reckless, moving too fast down the center of the classroom. All the glass vials and tubes clank loudly.

"Day after day, the teacher warns the student to slow down, but the student does not heed this directive, although the student always looks with great love at the teacher. Finally, one day the teacher has enough and says, 'You know, I have told you day after day to slow down, and you have not done so. Therefore, from now on, you will have to pay 50 cents for each tube and beaker that you break.' The student looks up at the teacher with great love and attempts to walk slowly, but halfway to the back of the room, the speed increases exponentially.

"The teacher hears a loud crash. Walking toward the closet, the teacher says, 'Now, this student will learn.' Then the teacher gasps when she sees the child. The child is embracing all the test tubes and beakers except one. The student looks up at the teacher with great love, and the teacher says, 'This is certainly a special child.'"

The nun then says, "Someday you will know the meaning of this parable, but first you must ask a great many people what they think it means. You will hear many answers, and there will be many good ones. However, when you hear the true meaning, you will know with certainty. You will feel through your entire body that it is the true answer. Nevertheless, you will continue telling the parable forever."

The nun responds, "Soon. Mine is the next stop after yours, Rose, so shortly I will be getting off the train. You get off on the very next stop, do you understand?"

The next stop comes far too quickly for Rose, but she stands up to say farewell. "Can I give you a hug?"

Mother says, "Of course you can!"

Rose hugs her. "I love you!"

And the nun returns the same, "Oh, I love you, too." That last hug of love lasts for Rose an awfully long time.

To Rose, who is seventeen years old, "soon" means the next week, but she does not discover the answer to the parable, to her chagrin, until age thirty-three. She tells the parable to many people, and each time, people give great responses, and she learns a great deal. She asks professors, priests, Hindus, Buddhists, atheists, agnostics, the educated, the uneducated, dozens and dozens—she almost gives up!

The old man leans toward Teresa to whisper in her ear, "So, tell me about the experience when you find your answer."

"You have no doubt, do you? You have great faith." Teresa dutifully continues the story.

"Thirsty in an arid and parched land without water
What pain is this? To see Divine Love so different from
human love.
How lonely now in human company I miss you my Lord
I miss you every moment every breath
Your love is greater than life."

ALTIERO, 1998

Chapter Nineteen

My Mary Magdalene

Rose is now completing her internship in psychology. She has befriended a girl who lives across the hall. Kim is a beautiful girl of eighteen who works as a call girl at night. One night, she stops by to borrow some sugar and tells Rose her entire life story.

Kim, a prostitute, a victim of incest, has suffered much. She also reveals the following, "Most people do not think that we pray, but I pray. I pray a rosary every night." The courage and honesty of this young woman are impressive. Rose and Kim become great friends. One evening, there is a knock on Rose's door. When Rose opens the door, Kim is standing there in her robe, having just taken a shower. All her makeup is off, and her face looks so innocent and young.

With a bottle of expensive perfume in one hand, she asks, "Where are your rosary beads? I want to spray them with perfume." What an incredible and sweet intention. Rose leads Kim to her rosary beads in a little pouch. Rose is sitting on a chair. Kim sits at Rose's feet and sprays the rosary, held delicately with her hand; Kim's humility and love are clearly apparent. Such an innocent face, so young without her heavy makeup, like a darling Mary Magdalene. Rose remembers her parable. Why not?

"Kim, I have a parable. I would like to tell you, and you tell me what you think it means, OK?" Kim remains seated on the floor, nodding in agreement and looking up at Rose in her chair. Like a child in elementary school, who is attentive to her teacher reading, Kim listens quietly, intently but does not say a single word; she only smiles with great love.

"Once, there was a chemistry teacher and an exceptional student. Oh, how the student loves the teacher. The student frequently looks up at the teacher with such great love that the teacher thinks, 'This is certainly a special child.'"

How peculiar that Kim is looking at Rose how the student looks at the teacher in the story.

"The student so loves the teacher that, to be helpful, the student stays after class. The student tries to help and often pushes a cart that holds vials and test tubes to the back of the room to store in the closet. However, the student is often reckless, going too fast down the center of the classroom, and the teacher hears the clanking of all the glass vials and tubes."

Rose pauses again. What if she could get Kim to stop using drugs?

"Day after day, the teacher warns the student to slow down, but the student does not heed this directive, although the student always looks with great love at the teacher. Finally, one day the teacher has enough and says, 'You know, I have told you day after day to slow down, and you have not done so. Therefore, from now on, you will have to pay 50 cents for each tube and beaker that you break.' The student looks up at the teacher with great love and attempts to walk slowly, but halfway to the back of the room, the speed increases intensely."

The reckless behavior makes Kim giggle, but she continues to listen and not say a word. "The teacher hears a loud crash. Walking toward the closet, the teacher says, 'Now, this student will learn.' Then the teacher gasps, seeing that the child embraces all the test tubes and beakers except one. The student looks up at the teacher with great love, and the teacher says, 'This is certainly a special child.'"

Finally, Rose finishes. "What does this story mean to you? The meaning of the parable?"

Bewildered, with the countenance of a young child, Kim says, "I don't get it. Who is the teacher, and who is the student?" There is such innocence in that one question—and so much truth. Suddenly, a shudder passed through Rose. After all those years and all the profound answers, this simple question is the answer.

With all certainty, Rose yells, "That is it! Kim, you got it! You got it! That is it!" Rose is now jumping up and down, and Kim joins in her celebration. Well, that is just how Kim is—so full of love.

Finally, Rose responds to Kim's question, "Right now, I am the student, and you are the teacher. The student can be teaching the teacher something, let us say, as an example of faith or love, while the teacher can be teaching discipline and strength. We never know who the student is or who the teacher is at any given moment. Therefore, even though I know the answer now, I will continue to tell the story to learn or teach. Oh, how wonderful! There is no room for pride here, just the love of discovery and sharing."

We never know who we are at any given moment as we interact with one another. We can be the student or the teacher. Therefore, after hearing the true meaning behind the parable, Rose knows she can continue to tell the story forever. The answer arrives through the innocent question of an incredibly young teacher whom she will hold close to her heart for the rest of her life.

Rose, never expecting to discover the truth to the parable, persists with discipline and tenacity. She learns many things from various people on her journey toward finding the meaning of the parable. Kim, being a servant of many and willing to spray the rosary with perfume as an offering to the Lord (whom she genuinely loves), holds a great treasure within her heart due to her long-suffering and persistence in prayer. Kim learns discipline from Rose. Rose learns about courageous love from Kim.

"The end!" Teresa speaks victoriously with a smile.

THE STUDENT IS THE TEACHER, AND THE TEACHER IS THE STUDENT

Then she asks the teacher, "Is it OK if I have some answers rather than just questions? What if life is full of teachers, and we are all students of love? The only true teacher is Jesus Christ. He helps us to learn from each other through the Holy Spirit. Could this be a true story about Rose? I wonder if that would make a difference to you. If so, why?"

Teresa finally looks up at the teacher; she is surprised to see tears flowing down his cheeks, although he wears a slight smile. He nods, and there appears to be an unfathomable depth of compassion within his eyes.

"It is a true story, and it is about you and your choice to love. What happens to Kim?"

"Oh, Kim stops using drugs with Rose's encouragement. She ends her area of work, and she goes to law school."

"So, Kim trusts you. She finds you to be competent, too. You lead her toward a new life. How?"

"Oh, for heaven's sake, I love her like a little sister. She is easy to love!"

"Yes indeed, for heaven's sake. Did it ever occur to you that you trusted Mother Superior very much because of the love directed toward you? In the same way, Kim trusted you. Would you like to discuss perfect trust tomorrow?"

Teresa places her hand on the teacher's shoulder with great love and gratitude. "Of course, I would!"

While walking home that day, Teresa wonders how the teacher knows what he knows, when he knows it, and why he knows it. There is something very mysterious about the older man. Will she ever acquire a fraction of that type of wisdom? Maybe once she retires? She thanks God for sending her this incredible storyteller to help her during her soul's night. How would it be if people continued to trust her as she trusts this wonderful older man? She shrugs her shoulders. "I can only hope they will."

After Teresa leaves, a bluebird watches the older man lift himself with his cane from the bench to depart with the sun. The twilight begins to shine through the heavens; the man looks up at the sky as if in prayer. The bird is emitting a beautiful song while it swings by him in graceful delight. It lands on his shoulder to sing in his ear. Imagine if someone had been watching! Someone is. Maggie and Mike are late returning from bird watching in the park, and both catch a glimpse of the older man with the friendly bird.

Mike says, "What the heck? I have never seen anything like that."

His wife responds, "Nor I," as they both look at each other in disbelief. Maggie is thinking, and her husband patiently watches his wife in deep thought.

She finally says, "Could he have anything to do with that woman?"

"Maybe so. Should we come back tomorrow?"

"Are you kidding? I would not miss it for the world. Something is going on here." The couple nods in silent agreement, and they head off for the evening.

Chapter Twenty

The Paraclete

Peeking around a bush are the two happily married people, who are pretty curious about the mysterious woman, who appears quite pleased talking to herself.

"Maybe she is an actress and rehearsing for a play," Maggie says.

"Maybe." Mike lifts his binoculars and looks at the peculiar woman. "Well, she is a bit of an introvert like our youngest daughter. So, would she want to be an actor?"

Maggie is displaying a dubious frown in response to her husband's suggestion. She then doubtfully shakes her head from side to side. "Mike, well, I don't know, that is just my best guess, and I don't want to say she is cray-cray."

Mike laughs. "You picked up that expression from our kids, and it is cute." He gives her a quick kiss on the lips, which pleases Maggie and still makes her blush. Yes, these are two outstanding people who are stumbling onto a mystery of sorts. Maggie considers, again, a meeting between the odd woman and that older man in the park, the one with the Saint Francis tendencies.

Teresa says, "How puzzling!" The bushes are trembling and alive with activity while concealing the couple. Hearing her statement, the two quickly duck out of sight. A bird flies from a branch. Ah, it is an animated bird causing the disturbance. He urgently lands beside Teresa, squawking up a storm. Mike and Maggie stealthily saunter away, clasping their mouth to contain their giggles. "Little bird, I am only walking by; what disturbs you?" The little bird cocks his head to one side and tweets, "There are people over there who are spying on you. They are bothering me as well."

"I wish I knew what you are saying, little one."

Teresa reflects on the discussion of the previous day and the teacher's question. "So, Kim trusted you. She thought you were competent too. You lead her toward a new life. How?" Teresa never answered that question. Kim trusts Teresa's heart and competency to help her, albeit as just a mere human. So, why does Teresa herself struggle with perfect trust in God? "Maybe I have more faith than I think," Teresa considers. "Perhaps I do."

The older man is watching a doe in the field who takes a genuine interest in him. It is surprising that the little doe comes up and settles by his feet.

"Teacher, how did you do that?"

He winks at Teresa. "She trusts me. It was a challenge for her, but like you, she does after a bit."

"It is because we can sense your gentle nature."

"That may well be, but trust still takes action on your part. It is a highly courageous act to trust. Upon entering this world, trust is a matter of survival. If you are fortunate enough to have an attentive and loving guardian, your early experiences with trust will be gentle and peaceful. Sadly, this is not the case for all births and all children. Some children have tough beginnings. The first bonds to another person are crucial to one's survival—some children who miss this bonding manifest a failure to thrive and even die.

"What happens to the children who survive this tragedy? What are they like as adults? Those with troubled childhoods do not consistently experience burgeoning security. However, some unfortunate souls become fortunate souls through the ameliorative efforts of an extended family member, a member of the clergy, a coach, a teacher, a mental health worker, a psychologist, or other such figures. (There are many possibilities.)

"If another human being shows kindness and compassion, a deprived individual can beat the odds. One in every three children, born under such harsh circumstances, comes out unscathed. Trust does not happen overnight and often takes time. Any young parent will tell you that it takes much work to calm and soothe her or his new infant. Over time, this trust develops through multiple experiences of getting one's needs met consistently. It is through this bond of trust that, over time, people develop an affinity for humankind and a sense of connectedness to the community. Some feel a connection to all creation, including the birds of the air and fish of the sea.

"Often, these people sense a higher calling and a connection to that beyond. Sometimes this experience of union arises unexpectedly and leaves the person stunned for the moment. Some mystics have called this experience a 'union with God,' which gives them great certainty. The experience of union is qualitatively different from the peak experience described by psychologists or by nature-lovers. In these spiritual states, God touches the soul so that the soul absolutely cannot doubt God's existence or the fact that each human life has a higher purpose."

"Teacher, I am familiar with that experience. It is as though the words, 'Be still, for I am your God' are spoken. Such unitive experiences give one the impression, for the moment, that all the concerns of the day, week, months, and years of one's life are trivial. Simply, nothing is more important than this moment of eternal truth in which the soul affirms God's existence without a doubt. Due to this most notable event, people think their entire life will change and that nothing will be as important—only to find, to their chagrin, that he or she must return to foolish thoughts and worldly pursuits soon afterward. Sadly, the soul is left to feel ashamed of itself as it returns to its human foolishness once again. All that changes is that one gains a sense of humility before the father, who lovingly says, 'Oh, my foolish people.'

"Questioning minds ask why some people have such experiences, and some do not. If I respond that this matter is God's prerogative, not ours, people scoff. They do not think that it is fair. Can you imagine that? Certain people are deciding for God what is reasonable. 'Oh, my foolish people' makes a lot of sense to me. Whether one receives it or not, we can be sure that this grace happens for a good reason. God's selection is for the best by divine providence. *Being the foolish person that I am*, I will also try to explain it.

"A union occurs for the benefit of a single soul and all of the human family. For example, when the Lord came to Paul at Damascus. By benevolence and his gracious divine plan, God helps Paul and humankind.

"I experienced perfect trust, unexpectedly, once."

"Tell me the story, Teresa."

At the time, I am at the hospital, just grabbing dinner before the café closes, and as I walk down the hall to enter the elevator, I hear a loud sound behind me in the corridor. A man yells, "What kind of God are you? I do not know why I am talking to you. I do not believe you! What kind of God would do what you did? If you were a good God, you would protect us."

Of course, I have edited this because the man uses some choice words that I would rather not repeat. All I can think at the time is: "Oh Lord, please let me get on the elevator before that potentially dangerous man reaches me." Then I recall it is Pentecost, celebrating the Holy Spirit's descent, and I am indebted to my Lord to function in the role to which he is about to call me.

I hear the man's voice, "Hey, lady!"

I hope he is not talking to me, but he is looking right at me when I turn around. So, what can I do? I say, "May I help you?"

"Can you tell me where the chapel is?"

"Sure, I know where the chapel is. It is not too far from here. I'll go with you."

Oh, I notice the man is in a wheelchair. He explains that he is a survivor of an accident.

He begins a rant. "I don't even care about this! I am worried about my friend in the critical care unit. Why would God do such a thing to such a nice guy?"

"But with all this anger, you still want to find the chapel to talk with him?"

"Someone suggested it, and I love my friend, and it is upsetting me. Why are you here at the hospital? Do you work here? Are you visiting someone?"

I take a deep breath before responding. I pray inwardly, "Oh Lord, you sent me to help this poor man, please help me do your will during this difficult time." I say to the man, "Yes, I am visiting; my husband is in the intensive care unit. They told me he is dying."

The man gasps. "Oh, my gosh, and you stop to help me? Do you love your husband?"

"Of course, I love him. I have been coming here for three months. I stay till midnight, drive home, go to sleep for three hours, and then they call me and wake me up at 3:00 AM to tell me he will die. So, I get out of bed and come here. I have been doing this for ninety days."

"They have told you for ninety days he is going to die, and he hasn't? How is he still alive, and why are you helping me? Don't you have enough on you?"

"No one can explain why he has not died. I know he is still fighting because we are very close. I also ask the Lord to give me some time. I pray a lot while I am here."

We arrive at a small chapel. I find a chair, and the gentleman, Tony, wheels himself in a while, tentatively looking around. "I don't know how to pray. I have never done it before. Can you teach me?"

"Just close your eyes and talk to him; you go first."

"Just talk to him. No rules? I did not know it was that easy." Tony closes his eyes. "God, are you there? I am Tony. I do not believe we have met, but I hear you are around. I am angry because my friend is in the ICU due to a car accident, and I do not know why you let this happen. He is a wonderful guy. I need help. Please, can you help me?" Tony starts to cry.

A tear is falling down Teresa's cheek, too.

He asks, "Was that right, or OK?"

"Tony, that is a beautiful prayer. Now, can I pray for you too?"

"Sure, I would like that."

"Heavenly Father, I am here with Tony, the one you love. I know you have not heard much from him. You hear many prayers from Christians, but they are often not this sincere and honest. I know you love those who come forward like Tony and tell you honestly what they think and feel; the vulnerable are before you. You prefer prayers like Tony's more than the superficial ones of those without feelings of love in their heart. Please help Tony know your love and how much you love him so that he knows the peace you give me even during this very dark hour."

I open my eyes, and there is Tony with tears and a smile. "I did not know it could be like that, prayer. Talking like he is your friend." Tony bids farewell and, with great strength, moves back down the hall. He does not know me, but again he trusts me, and I trust God to help me do the job he has sent me to do. I trust God altogether that day. It is a gift, an experience of union.

I hear that, from those who receive lavish gifts, we can expect much in return. Therefore, it could be genuinely daunting to receive this or any grace. I do not know if I can ever express enough gratitude to God for this gift. A man I was afraid of turns out to feel like a brother I love—so amazing!

It is not an easy task to explain God's existence, nor is it as successful as one might think given the numerous reports of "fortunate" or "unfortunate" people. Suppose a person, hearing this story, is familiar with the experience of union or grace or soul searching (displayed by Tony). In that case, he or she might nod with a silly grin of affirmation. However, if a person has not had a unitive experience, she or he might be thinking, "Yeah, real nut case!" or "Religious fanatic!" As Tony, some people might be likely to believe in such things, but they find it hard to believe because they do not happen to or for them. Those people who believe without having seen have great spiritual faith, which I admire and envy. Because I, too, am foolish.

Teresa gives a heavy sigh of resignation.

"Teresa, you say it was Pentecost. Did anything else unusual happen that day?"

"It is strange that you should ask about other miracles. There is another that happened on the elevator that day. Shall I tell you the story?"

"Please."

Leaving Tony, I get on the elevator. There is only one other person there. He is in the corner weeping. Of course, I remark, "You are so sad." Many people say, "Are you OK?" but it is apparent that he is not. He is hurting.

The man looks up. "My wife is dying. There's no brain activity, and I am going now to take her off life support."

"I am so sorry. I can tell you love your wife, and this is so hard for you."

"It is, it is. I should pray, but I cannot. I just can't."

"Would you like me to pray for you?"

The man looks hopeful. "I mean, I know she is gone from here, but I want her journey to be OK so that she can go to heaven peacefully."

"I will do this right now." The man clasps his head and bows.

"Heavenly Father, please take your daughter into your loving care where she can experience joy, not of this world. She will be bringing with her heart the incredible love of this dear man. Please comfort and bring peace to this lovely man who knows how to love. Please help him understand how much you love him. He carries her love within his heart. Please take away any apprehension and replace it with peace. Amen."

"Thank you, thank you so much!" and the man departs.

In the late evening, upon entering the elevator again, a man stands in the corner. He has a white lab coat on, and he is a doctor. He, too, is tearful; his pain is apparent.

"Doctor, you are having a tough day."

"Yes, I am. We just had to take a woman off life support, and her husband was there. It was rough. We did everything we could do. I wish there were more, but that was all we could do. He loves his wife. He continues to grieve this loss."

"I think I spoke to the man this morning about this."

"Are you a family member?"

"No, he just asked me to pray for them."

"That's unusual and peculiar. I mean for you to talk to me by chance on this elevator."

"No, Doctor, I have not been on the elevator all day."

The humorous comment causes him to give a half-smile. "I know."

"Doctor, my husband has been in the ICU for ninety days now because both lungs have collapsed. I just want you to know that when we go through these horrendous things, you are the type of doctor we want around our family members because you care. We may not be able to say it at the time, but we do. I would like to thank you for being such a good doctor."

Now I see a full smile, and he says, "Thank you, I appreciate that."

I watch an excellent doctor walk toward his car.

Oh great, I have missed my garage floor. Now the elevator goes all the way up again. This time a man enters the elevator. He is unusual because he appears in a fine suit with a perfectly crisp white shirt that is so pristine it sparkles. There is tremendous strength in him and an angelic quality; he is black and has perfect facial features. His face is symmetrical, and he is the ideal weight for his height. He is silent and looking straight ahead.

When we reach my floor, the angelic man turns to me and says, "May God continue to be beside you, all around you, and in you."

I look at him and nod like this is a typical conversation for an elevator.

He then says sternly with the strength of an archangel, "Do you understand?

"Yes." I walk off the elevator and feel this incredible strength, and I know it is Pentecost. I have trusted God all day through the grace of the Holy Spirit. I cannot do that type of thing alone and not always.

The teacher glances at the lower lip pouting thing that Teresa is doing and withholds a laugh. He helps her out of her funk. He notices a tiny tear in the shoulder of his tweed coat. The gesture reminds Teresa of the needle and thread in her coat pocket. She pulls it out to view.

"I've meant to sew that for you, but I keep forgetting. Can you trust me to do this? Will you be cold?" The older man takes his coat off and hands it to Teresa with gratitude. Teresa's hands are small and gentle. She takes great care in this task.

"Teresa, it sounds like you do at times leave your fear behind and just let go and let God, as they say. You are learning perfect trust, and you have come a long way through suffering. I have a story for you."

As usual, that brings a great grin to her face and makes the teacher chuckle.

"I am a servant

Of

The Lord."

ALTIERO, 1998

Chapter Twenty-One

Original Sin

THE STORY OF THE DOCTORAL STUDENT AND THE LOTTERY TICKET

Jill is a struggling doctoral student who takes her studies quite seriously. She has been studying all day, and, at this point, she knows that she needs a break. Jill's break usually includes a quick stroll with an opportunity for distraction. Today she finds herself in rural Carbondale, Illinois, in a small row of shops that could hardly be called a mall. She notices a small theater. A movie would be great! The matinees are cheaper, and the sign indicates the cost is four dollars. Hopefully, she has that. However, to her disappointment, only one dollar is in her purse.

"I guess our Lord does not want me to see a movie today," she concludes while continuing her walk, a bit slower this time. What can be done with a single dollar nowadays? Jill spots a candy store. Believe it or not, all the candy is more than a dollar. All that is selling for one dollar is a lottery ticket. Jill pauses. She will buy a lottery ticket. If she wins, she could become a wealthy woman, and life would be different. As she passes her dollar to the cashier, she silently prays, "Lord, if winning all this money will corrupt me, please do not let me win." As the dollar bill leaves her hand, she has a sudden feeling that, indeed, it would corrupt her. So, she knows that she will not win, but she lets go of the money anyway.

The man turns his back on her, runs the ticket, and says, "You won! You won!"

"That's surprising; what did I win?"

The man meekly smiles as he sees the amount, which is only four dollars.

"That is wonderful! Now I can go to the movie."

The cashier finds her response to the small amount pleasantly surprising. Jill is amazed by this perfect surprise and windfall. She walks off, this time quite quickly, to catch the next showing. As she enters the darkened theater, she looks up to talk to God. "What, you couldn't spring for some popcorn?"

As soon as the thought passes her mind, she feels great shame. She could have been grateful, but instead, she offers resentment. "Alas," Jill thought, "I may never be wealthy, thinking like that, which is a good thing." She timidly smiles as she experiences the comforting care of a wiser being, the one she loves, her God.

DISCERNMENT: HEARING GOD

The teacher turns to Teresa, "Have you ever received not what you want, but what you need? How did it work out?"

Teresa laughs and says two words, "Yea, you!"

The teacher holds up two fingers to indicate two words and looks at her in a questioning way, "Only two words?"

Teresa gives him a mischievous grin. She wants to play. To indicate intense thought, the older man puts his thumb, and index finger on his chin then slides his fist under his chin as in Rodin's sculpture *The Thinker*. He then points his finger at Teresa, suggesting that he wants more than a two-word answer. "Have you ever received what you needed rather than what you wanted?"

Teresa blurts out a response, "Jill and I are a lot alike. Well, I want my best friend back. As I said when I met you, it at first was a big bummer but, if that had not happened, I might not have gotten to know you or even have seen you."

"That would be terrible. Yes, indeed. Not meet my precious Teresa. An unacceptable event."

"Both Jill and I struggle with letting go and letting God—you know, perfect trust. Does it have anything to do with discernment or knowing when to let go?"

Teresa appears to have found her voice again and elaborates upon her question. "Many people discuss their difficulties with discernment. I often hear statements such as: 'I just can't tell what the Lord wants me to do!' Often, many nonbelievers think, 'Oh, for heaven's sake, try making your own decision! Try using that brain that you have between your two ears!' You know what? They might be right. When did people start expecting to be spoon-fed because they want to do what the Lord wills them to do? Often people say, 'Well, Lord, should I do that or this? It is your call!' Then, there is a long silence and even no answer at all. People might fear that they have lost a connection, like a dropped call from their cell phones. 'Are you there?' Again, no answer. 'Why?' Maybe, some people have the gift of discernment more than others."

"Yes, some do have that appearance. However, it could be some people have more confidence in their decisions, at least. They are more courageous and bolder in their formulations and opinions, but are they always right? Perfect trust has more to do with humility than discernment. Do you hear more about their mistakes or successes? Who is to say what counts as a mistake or success anyway?"

"God decides that. So, back to square one, discernment arrives in any chosen person when they are part of his divine plan. When Peter cut that guy's ear off, it was not part of the divine plan, though he believed it to be right at the time. This uncertainty, or not knowing, may be part of the plan. An admission of uncertainty and not knowing may humble us to trust in God more. Jill trusts in the Lord when she asks God not to make her wealthy if it would hurt her spiritually. Minutes later, she questions his decision by wondering about popcorn. How exactly do we lose that trust?"

"During infancy, through touching, seeing, hearing, tasting, and smelling, people learn about their existence. Interactions via the senses encourage separation from the environment and people. As people become older, losing track of their souls, they quickly abandon God. The feeling of unity departs due to original sin. However, the separation allows for free will and the choice to love and even to return."

"I am hopeful but find that puzzling." Teresa takes some time to sort out this enigma. "In some way, we must forget that he loves us. We drift so far into the world of our senses. Curious about that which is physically tangible and fascinated by our new experiences and knowledge, it is as if some great deceiver orchestrates a symphony of distractions to divert us from God and his love for us. We forget to be grateful."

ORIGINAL SIN

"That is true, Teresa. There is a lie within the fiction. Some assumptions cannot be proved or disproved. Within this reality hides the master of deceit, the prince of all lies, waiting to ambush souls. He began this evil plan in the garden of Eden. 'God does not want you to eat from the tree, and *he is withholding what you need* to feel and be better.' The senses get the best of Eve when she observes the ripe, juicy fruit. The perfect trust in God is lost.

The God who so lovingly offers his children what is best seems absent. *The devil convinces them that they are not happy, so they are not truly loved.* It is the belief, not the reality, which is the lie within the fiction. Trust in God and his divine love is marred by the devil's plot, and the evil one is thrilled."

Teresa observes, "So, we take command to feel powerful. We are afraid to feel lost and lose control. Our trust in God is lost. My desire for discernment may evince this too."

"People make multiple assumptions that are choices, not absolute scientific facts, in this construction of reality. People are finite within an infinite creation. They do not have the entire picture. Some people feel more secure with merely knowing what they know through science because they are intelligent and knowledgeable about physical creation, which the senses can measure and perceive. Others are uncomfortable with such limitations and prefer to look at the mystery, an infinite design and not merely their sensorium, to construe their reality. These different ways of looking at the world often cause division, hatred, and conflict, although such outcomes are not inevitable. When trust in God is lost, mistrust in others follows in consequence. It is strange how the mad scientist and the religious zealot can appear out of nowhere, having been previously very rational and compassionate people. When the devil can destroy the trust between people and God, as he did with Adam and Eve, he can harm their faith in each other, as he did between Adam and Eve. The devil wants to destroy love. Teresa, many people's hearts harden, and they direct so much hate toward that which they do not understand. Pride sows mistrust, anger, and even hatred."

Great sadness fills Teresa's eyes. "Yes, and look what happened to my Jesus!"

The teacher is quiet for a while and looks at Teresa as if studying her. No, not that; it is as if he is making an account of her heart. She is trying to make sense of this when he finally speaks, "Teresa, you get very anxious when you do not know what to do for God. You get a bad case of scruples. I have a story for you."

What? How does he know all that?

"I would like to tell you about Mary, an adorable little girl who pouts just like you!"

Chapter Twenty-Two

Highly Sensitive, Purity of Heart

Mary is only four years old. So, she likes to look around the big tree in the backyard while her mother sits close by with the neighbor, drinking coffee. It is a beautiful spring day, the sun is shining, and the birds are singing, but suddenly Mary catches sight of a small robin's egg on the ground by the tree. She looks closely at the egg, hoping to put the egg back in the nest because the mother is crying above. To her horror, she discovers that the tiny, speckled egg, with the golden yellow yolk, is dripping out onto the bright green grass.

Mary supposes the baby has died, and the mother will never see her baby again. She first begins to whimper, but quickly her tears come, and then wails emit from her lips. Both her mother and the neighbor are startled and run over to Mary. Her mother thinks she may have been stung by a bee, and she is confused by her daughter's reaction to the broken egg.

"Now, don't be silly. It is just an egg. Why are you crying?"

"Mommy, the baby is dead!" The mommy does not see. She is looking but cannot see.

The neighbor bends down to Mary's level and says, "My, my, you are a sensitive little girl. I wonder what you are going to be when you grow up." Mary does not understand why neither of the grown-ups is as upset about the poor baby, and she feels so alone. Mary's temperament does not change, and within two years, she finds herself in Sunday school.

Mary loves her Sunday school class and the teacher, who is the priest. She is in first grade. When the priest tells stories about Jesus and the Bible, his beautiful face radiates. Father Cauwe must be like Jesus because his eyes sparkle with great love. He mostly tells delightful stories, but this day is different, very different, and very sad.

Father Cauwe tells the story of Judas and how he betrays Jesus and then actually hangs himself from a tree. Mary can visualize the entire scene: Jesus in the garden and the soldiers coming with Judas, who kisses Jesus on the cheek. The eyes of Jesus droop with sadness as Judas backs away. Does Jesus know that, because of the betrayal, Judas will wind up feeling such guilt that he will harm himself? Mary grasps the entire story and even sees it play out in her imagination. She is despairing. What a terrible tale. Overcome with emotion; Mary cries out, "Oh, I feel sorry for Judas!"

Gasps follow harsh accusatory statements from her classmates. "You're as bad as he is." "He killed Jesus! You should not feel sorry for him." "Do you hate Jesus?" They yell, "Boo!" and throw paper at her. Her peers are angry.

Then for the very first time, Father Cauwe's face is full of anger as he yells, "Stop! I do not ever want to see you act that way again. That is how Jesus felt. Sorry for Judas and sorry for all of us." The class moans and falls silent. Given their trust for Father Cauwe, they are ashamed.

Father Cauwe looks down at Mary, who looks up at him with tears in her eyes. Her classmates must hate her, and he gently says, "You see, Mary, I too feel sorry for Judas." He then gives her a beautiful smile, and his eyes sparkle just like Jesus's eyes. Father Cauwe looks at Mary again and says, with great love, "You are a special child."

Mary smiles. Her heart fills with love and joy. She is with Father Cauwe, and Jesus is with Father Cauwe, too. Most importantly, Mary is no longer alone, looking at a broken robin's egg, feeling misunderstood.

The older man asks Teresa, "In light of the neighbor's question, what will Mary be when she grows up? Mary, as an adult, will become someone with whom people can confide when they need help. Even you might confide in her. Would you? Why or why not?"

Teresa is looking wide-eyed at the teacher as if in shock. How does he know all of that? That exact thing happened to her as a child. She loved that priest. The teacher seems to know about that. She is about to speak, but he signals to her to be quiet.

"Shh! I have more to say about Mary."

Chapter Twenty-Three

Angry at God

Throughout Mary's childhood, she learns a great deal from Father Cauwe. For example, she grows in patience for her father's bad temper and finds a hidden blessing in most things. One day, she misses the school bus, which causes her father to rant and demand that she walk the five miles to school. Mary is thirteen by then, so she thinks she can manage on foot. On the way to school, she passes the church. Father Cauwe is serving at the 6:30 a.m. Mass. What an opportunity to go to Mass before school and have time with her beloved Father Cauwe. Mary's routine continues every school day. She walks two and a half miles to church, two and a half miles to school, and five miles back from school. Mary comes to enjoy hiking.

Mary and the priest are best friends for three more years, until her sixteenth birthday, when he becomes very ill. He had been a prisoner of war early in life, at which time he contracted yellow fever. Although Father Cauwe is only in his mid-forties, he looks like he is in his seventies. These last couple of months, he needs to rest on her shoulder just to make it into the church. Mary always smiles as they hobble in because she does not want him to know that she is anxious about him. One day, as she catches up to him, he becomes so exhausted that he cannot continue the journey without her. He must have eyes in the back of his head because his arm is out to put around her shoulder. "I need your help today, my special child."

He is heavier today, thankfully, for that keeps her from crying. "I will bear this cross," she decides. "I will not cry in front of my best friend." Inside, her heart is breaking. It is as if she were going with him to the last Mass he would ever say.

Shortly after the assembly at the church, he dies. Mary weeps a thousand tears; the little girl who has cried about the robin's egg feels alone once more. There is such pain when the priest dies, tremendous grief, followed by intense anger.

"You did not tell me you have the gift of prophecy, Teacher. I had no idea. Does that happen for you all the time or just sometimes? I have it sometimes, too, but not like that. Entire pieces of my life. How could you know? Yes, I remember the robin's egg, the angry students, and the death of my best friend."

"Yes, and you are outraged like Mary."

Chapter Twenty-Four

My Best Friend

Mary is furious at God. He took her Father Cauwe away. How dare he be so cruel and heartless? She is a good girl and even goes to church six days a week. It seems like God has lost his mind. Mary feels so hurt and betrayed. She cannot even count on God. Now a crippling weakness comes over her, making it impossible to walk. Her best friend is gone when she needs him most. To whom can she talk now? Mary leaves the house, slamming the door. Her temper, consistently strong, is much worse today than her father's because he *never* yells at God.

Mary marches down the block in a fury, muttering aloud, "What kind of God are you? How could you do such a thing? Heartless! What did I do to you? What did Father Cauwe do to you? How could you? After how much we have loved you." Suddenly, Mary wants to hurt God back. Whether he can send a bolt of lightning through the air to kill her, in retribution, does not matter, and she does not care. If so, she would be dead with Father Cauwe. Fine! Mary looks up at the sky, holding her fist to the heavens. "I don't believe in you. There! I don't believe in you anymore." Inhaling, she waits for the lightning bolt.

Absolutely nothing happens. Mary looks up at the sky in confusion. A gentle wind caresses the hair on her face. A kind voice enters her soul. "My little child, if you do not believe in me, to whom are you talking?"

Mary does not expect that reaction. Is he making a joke? This response catches her off guard. She awaits anger and cruelty but receives a kind, loving, and rational response from God instead. She drops her head as a gesture of repentance. "My God, my God, I am talking to my best friend." She feels great shame, and tears gush from her eyes. Mary no longer feels betrayed by God, nor does she suffer from a crippling weakness preventing her from walking. As she slowly walks home, she realizes she will never be alone because her best friend is the creator of all that is, was, and will be: the incredible unexpected who makes *exceptional exceptions*.

Teresa addresses the teacher. "Yes, this is all true. That is exactly right. What you describe of Mary is what happened to me. But you were not there—your gift is so powerful. I was so grateful that day and delighted by such love and kindness. I expected pride like mine. Instead, God gave me what I need. God can make an exceptional exception because God is perfect love."

"God's response softens your heart again, which is beginning to harden," the teacher remarks. "And you are right. He gives you what you need. God makes an *exceptional exception* for humanity. After the original sin, God gives his dear children a second chance to know how he loves them and sends his only son to show love's depth. The son entirely trusts the father. He loves and accepts the extreme act of sacrifice, leading lambs to trust God's eternal love again. You know, Teresa, he had plans for you, great things to do for God."

"What things, teacher?"

"You were to become a seamstress."

"Wait. What? I am a psychologist. I did not know that. I thought my calling was to be a psychologist. I can't even sew that well."

"You are a seamstress. For compassion is the thread of your needle, and you mend broken hearts. You did a good job on my tweed coat, as well." He now takes a deep breath, "Remember, Teresa, you get what you need, not always what you want."

"Oh, no, what is it?"

"Tomorrow will be our last meeting. I have somewhere else I must go, something else to do."

The broken robin's egg and the loss of Father Cauwe are happening all over again. What dread and disappointment! Usually, Teresa would become angry and have a fit to lift herself out of her sorrow. However, if she did that again, could she ever get it right? This perfect trust thing?

The teacher is looking at her soulfully. "All right, I will see you tomorrow."

Impulsively, she hugs him and runs off so that he will not see her cry. It suddenly strikes her, and she slows her pace. If he is so gifted, he will know she is heartbroken. He has not said anything. She tells herself, "I can do this. The teacher is right. I can. I can. There is pain, but this time it can be different. I will accept this suffering for the glory of God."

Chapter Twenty-Five

Love One Another as I Have Loved You

FRIENDS IN A TIME OF NEED

The next day Teresa slowly strolls to the park. She is forgetting something but cannot bring it to mind. The slumbering sun hides behind a billowy cloud in an overcast sky. The eagle flies toward the storm to rise above the upcoming cacophony of thunderous lightning, as eagles do. While delaying the inevitable storm, the sun peeks out at Teresa just to check if all is well. Although she wants to be brave for the teacher, as she had been for Father Cauwe so many years ago, there is a heaviness in her heart. The melancholy wail of a dove calls in the distance. A mother bird is calling for her child, or an egg has fallen from the nest? That is all it takes for the flood gate to open and the tears to fall. Well, she cannot let the teacher see her like this. She must pull herself together.

Meanwhile, Maggie and Mike are entering the park, and they see her crying.

"Mike, oh, no! Something must be happening to her!"

Maggie's compassion is clearly noted by her husband.

"Maybe, Maggie, she did not get the part?"

Maggie shakes her head. "Point not well taken, Mike. You don't shed that kind of sorrow for something like that."

Although Mike knows what Maggie will do, he asks anyway, "What should we do?"

Maggie starts to march toward Teresa. "Mike, we need to comfort her."

"You know, she might just be nuts."

"Mike, I don't care."

Mike loves his wife's kind heart and maternal instinct. What a lucky man!

Teresa is leaning against the park fence when Maggie arrives at her side. "I am sorry, but I can't help but notice that you are upset."

"I am very, very sad." Teresa is blowing her nose on her crumpled tissue.

"What's up, ladies?" Mike surprises both women. Maggie glares at Mike because of his lack of sensitivity. After Teresa recovers from the shock of Mike's sudden approach, which is so out of place, she starts hysterically laughing.

Maggie, with a sigh of relief, chuckles, as well. "That's my Mike!" Mike just grins, looking quite proud of himself. There is something Teresa likes about this couple, something special.

Maggie puts a hand on Teresa's shoulder. "Would you like to share the pain? I am all ears."

"I am saying goodbye today to a wonderful friend, and I am afraid that sometimes I get so attached to people—it breaks my heart when they leave."

"Oh, but that is sweet. You have such a kind heart, and there is nothing wrong with that."

"Thank you; it is just that it causes me such pain."

Maggie thinks for a while and points with her index finger for emphasis, "It was Saint Teresa of Avila who said something like Jesus loves most those who suffer and that he allows their suffering for a reason. I cannot remember the reason. I am not sure where that came from because I am not that religious."

Mike is surprised at his wife's comment, too. "Yeah, she usually does not talk like that. However, to continue with her inconsistency, I recall it is because Jesus suffers so that we can find the road to compassion and charity.

In short, to get close to the heart of Jesus, which is gentle, kind, and meek. We must suffer when learning to love."

Maggie turns to her husband. "Where did that come from?"

"I don't know. This experience is weird—I caught what you have. You know, we made that couples thing, the retreat at the church a while back. Maybe someone mentioned it then."

Teresa is finding their conversation quite entertaining—they are trying to rationalize away the presence of the Holy Spirit in their hearts. There is a miracle, however, because her faith is different now, and it is a great comfort to know that great people all around her can be teachers or students. The realization gives her a greater trust in God, which is just what she needs. She abruptly stands up and hugs both Maggie and Mike. "Thank you for this. Whatever you did and said and why—thank you."

Both Maggie and Mike are smiling with relief. "Are you going to be late for the last meeting with your friend?"

"Oh, yes! I better run."

Before they can say a word more, she is hurrying down the path.

"Do you want to find out who this friend is?" Mike queries.

"Of course," Maggie says and picks up her pace.

Teresa's stomach is growling, and that is when she remembers that she has forgotten to eat breakfast.

Oddly, when she arrives, the teacher is holding a loaf of homemade bread. "You're just in time to share my bread." He breaks the loaf in half and lovingly hands it to her, raising his eyebrows. "Let's see if you like it." The bread is unusual, with its perfect color, soft texture, and crisp crust. It is terrific, or she is starving, or both. The teacher laughs, "Quiet this morning, or is the bread that good?"

Teresa is stuffing her mouth, "That good!" She has a large piece of bread in her mouth, making them both laugh even more.

"Okay, I will talk about the role of suffering in people's lives while you listen and eat." Teresa wants to tell the teacher that she has just been talking about that subject with two other people, but she cannot because her mouth is full.

The teacher begins. "Imagine that there is a creator of this vast existence. Do you think that such a charitable entity is out to get you? The one who gives you all creation to learn from and a free will for deciding which lessons you will learn first?"

Teresa finally swallows her last piece of bread. "A priest once told me that every time you say what God is, you also say what he is not. If you say God is merciful, yes, God is merciful, but also not merciful. He is not merciful by human standards, nor is he merely compassionate by a limited human perspective. The finite cannot explain the infinite, nor can one pour the ocean into a single shell. I am not saying that a healthy fear of the creator is not warranted. We are talking about the vast everything (and what is not). It is simply disrespectful to try to define or understand the mind of God. Let us just say that God is the unexpected, relative to whatever we think God is or may be at any given time. Likely, an infinitely merciful intelligence, relative to nothing and existing outside of time and space, is incomprehensible. Are we merely specks of dust floating upon a voice of uncertainty and diminishing into silence?"

"Teresa, that is quite a mouthful—no pun intended. It is quite profound."

"I learn from the best." She winks at the teacher as she gives the compliment.

He gives a startled smile. "This mystery will not be understood by the finite brain, nor by trying to grapple with the creator. However, the acts that you think are great, indeed, by human standards, might not be deemed so by the creator. Small acts in the world's eyes—simple gifts of kindness and charity—are valuable acts that have beautiful repercussions within the human family throughout creation. People experience life and the unexpected, infinite revelation of God. It is the unforeseen that reminds people of their vulnerability, and total separation is not a good idea. The living truth in the experience of love has meaning, and it is life changing. Which reminds me of Tom and his Aunt Beatrice."

Chapter Twenty-Six

You Have Forgotten How Much I Love You!

Tom's Aunt Beatrice buys him thick red Christmas socks every year. They are not only red; the socks have the toes attached, which makes them suitable attire for a martian. Did she expect him to wear these? She has undoubtedly lost one or two marbles from her little gray head—Tom grunts and wonders why other people's aunts send "normal" gifts. Tom complains about these garish gifts to his mother every year. "Mom, why does she do this year after year? What do I have that will match these crazy socks? The kids will tease the heck out of me at school."

His mother, being the good mother she is, advises, "Accept them gratefully. You will be glad you did when she passes away." She then suggests that he put them in a shoebox up in his room. He thinks that is a good idea, out of sight and out of mind.

When Tom is twenty-one years old and away at college, he receives a call from home, stating that his aunt has died. With his friend Frank, Tom goes home on a cold wintry day, broken-hearted, for his aunt's funeral. She was eccentric for sure, but he has grown quite fond of her unorthodox ways over the years. Tom is getting dressed when he realizes that he has been in such a hurry, leaving school, that he has forgotten his socks. He asks Frank if he has an extra pair and, to his chagrin, discovers that his friend has forgotten his socks, as well.

"What are we going to do?" they exclaim in unison. Tom spots the old shoebox in the corner of his closet. He then grabs some of the red socks out of the box and hastily throws a pair at his friend.

Frank is amazed. "Hey, cool socks, man! With toes. It is 20 below out there. Here, I thought you were too rigid a person, and you have these amazing socks for a funeral."

Tom replies, "We're wearing these in her honor." The gesture touches Tom's mother. His friend Frank—well, he makes the socks all the rage at school. Furthermore, every Christmas, Tom dons a pair of red socks to warm his toes and heart.

"Tom matures through suffering the loss," Teresa explains. "He knows his aunt loves him but feels her love more in its absence; he can feel the difference. I wonder if Adam and Eve feel similarly after being cast out of the garden away from their father."

The teacher explains, "Often, people receive gifts that they think they do not want. They may consider these gifts as if they were crosses, burdens, or even punishments. Life is the greatest gift. If a gift symbolizes the relationship between two people, what is Tom's gift, and how does he receive the gift at first? If a baby is one of the gifts that symbolize the relationship between God and people, what is a person's offering to God when they choose to accept the gift?" Teresa is sad because she has some close friends who have had abortions, and they feel a significant loss afterward.

"Oh, but teacher, are you saying that those who choose abortion are ungrateful? I don't think they mean to do that when they make that decision."

"It is not prudent to generalize in that way and say all are ungrateful. They are told about science to assuage their conscience, and they believe in science, and some are in difficult situations. They are afraid and feel that they have no one to turn to for comfort. Many individuals do not have the intention to be ungrateful for the gift of life. Many do not understand that the miracle of life includes a soul. Sometimes, after the loss, through miscarriage or abortion, women feel an absence, a significant loss. This sorrow is not occurring so that they can feel unloved by God or hopeless. All that comes from God is a gift to the individual and the human family, even suffering. His gifts are given through merciful love, even if the human destiny of that soul is a corporal loss. This gift is a gift of love, and the loss of a little one is of great significance. Their souls return to God. The conception of life had and has a place in the divine plan." Teresa notices a nest in a tree behind the teacher's head. Two baby birds poke their heads up to see what is going on. Teresa finds the teacher's words comforting because she has lost two girls through miscarriages. The mother bird comes back to feed her young, and the two babies sing for joy. I wonder if my babies will sing for joy when I return?

"Teresa, women who miscarry and those who have abortions suffer greatly, and God is sad for them, as well. Often, they feel bad and even get angry because they think religious fanatics make them feel like monsters. Some God-fearing people proudly think their belief in life's sanctity also suggests they should be judge and jury in every situation. They become offended as if they are God. Some even bomb abortion clinics or support the death penalty. Sadly, they even think they are better than other people who have abortions. Some even put horrendous pictures of babies aborted on the automobiles of women who have just had miscarriages. Others treat those who have had miscarriages and wanted a baby as if they are fools. They ridicule their grief saying, 'Why are you so upset about a fertilized egg?' Many people pass judgments on entire groups, not recognizing that change occurs through everyone's change of heart. Terrible political arguments ensue as pride grows on both sides, while compassion disappears because each side demonizes the other side. The master of deceit and the prince of all lies is happiest at those moments. *His goal is to remove love from every interaction*." The sorrow on the older man's face is quite apparent.

"The truth, Teresa, is that manufactured laws often interfere with people consulting the counselor, the Holy Spirit, when facing such difficulties. The counselor is the first to turn to with difficult decisions."

Some of what the teacher describes stings Teresa's heart as she recalls the plight of two clients who had abortions. "May I tell you a story about one of my clients who had an abortion?"

The teacher says, "Please do."

"There was once a young lady, just thirteen years old and, while living in poverty, she came to the unit due to a suicide attempt and an attempt to self-abort her baby. As I am sitting there with the girl, I realize she has a secret, and Jesus reveals the secret to my soul, which almost makes me cry. He tells me that the young girl is a victim of incest. She has tried to self-abort the baby, and she almost dies. The desperate woman tries to protect her father, an alcoholic, who is all she has for a family.

"I remember my great love for the little girl who is a protector. I understand, since I have once taken the similar role of protecting my father, though for a different reason. I sat at the table with the young lady and a psychiatrist involved in her care. 'I know you are protecting someone, someone you love.' The young lady looks bewildered. How do I know her secret?

"The teenager begins to cry, 'How do you know?' The psychiatrist in the room is surprised and finds nothing in the progress notes to suggest such information.

"I continue to listen to my heart; the message from Jesus, my beloved friend, is as follows. 'She thinks I have forgotten her because of what she did. She thinks I am no longer with her, but she believes in me. Help my little lamb know that I am with her always.' I say to her, 'He hears your prayers and loves you. He does not want you to be alone. He is with you, and he loves you.'

"With those final words, the girl begins to wail in relief, begging for reassurance, 'Are you sure? Are you sure?' After reassuring the teenager, the psychiatrist and I, with great compassion for this child, with tears in our eyes, sit with her as she cries an ocean of sorrowful, soothing tears. We can help this little lamb with the grace of God."

The teacher nods, reflecting on Teresa's story before he speaks, "No one told this little one that she was a murderer and that she should go to jail. Instead, Teresa, you were told by the Holy Spirit to tell her she is loved and give her what she needed, not what she wanted, which was to die. It is a battle with original sin, believing that God does not endlessly love her and does not give her what she needs. He never withholds his love when you turn to him in sorrow with contrite hearts and repentant spirit. The counselor was guiding you, Teresa, in comforting this fragile, lovable young woman."

"So true, teacher, I felt such love; it must come from God. I wish everyone knew that no matter what your choices are, God does not hate you! He does not call you a murderer, he does not blame you for a miscarriage, and he does not condemn through human laws. Our laws and interpretations are often morbid aberrations of truth denigrated by the tree of knowledge, original sin. Therefore, our laws can have great errors, for example, slavery and oppression. God's love is redemptive and perfect. I have another experience that I would like to share.

"In the second situation, a suicidal woman comes to my office. 'I have had seven abortions, and I believe God will damn me to hell.' As a Catholic, she visited a priest, but she could not receive the priest's mercy and kindness. The young woman, a victim of incest, physical abuse, and multiple sexual assaults, only knew pain, cruelty, and a lack of compassion. This gentle lady is one of the vulnerable wounded, surviving through a lifetime of horror. She knows what a lack of kindness feels like, and she believes she has shown the same to her children. She is conflicted about compassion and her lost children.

"My heart bleeds for this sweet lady. So, I quietly ask for the help of my beloved. Entering my heart, he says, 'I once banished seven demons from Mary Magdalene, remember?' At first, I find the message cryptic, but then I know. There is such great pain on this woman's face, and she appears to be waiting for harm from me rather than help. For her, there is only a cruel and heartless world.

"'You are in such great misery. It seems unbearable. I want you to hold on for your children's sake.' The woman looks confused. I explain. 'Children like these have a martyred baptism according to canon law in the Catholic church. Martyred means they are saints in heaven now. They love and watch over you. What I think you can do is to name each child one at a time. Go for each child separately to confession, each on a different day. Let the priest know that you love this child. Let the priest know that you would like Jesus to tell them you love them. Because you do, I can see that.'

"The reasoning appears to resonate in this young woman's heart. The cloak of despair leaves and reveals the unexpressed love she has, causing pain. She begins to cry, 'I like that, and I want to do that! Those are my babies!'

"I explore her thoughts and feelings to ascertain that she wants to stay alive for her babies. The lady is smiling now and hopeful. The evil one has been after this woman since birth to destroy her capacity to love. She comes through victoriously from the battle. When returning to her future sessions, she often wears brightly colored dresses, and her face reflects the mercy of God. Her self-esteem dramatically improves.

"As you said, teacher, change occurs by softening each heart tenderly, lovingly, and patiently. A psychologist may say that the healing happens because she has had seven positive interactions with a priest after being hurt by so many men, and that has been therapeutic. A clergy person may say that seven demons have been persecuting her. They know her potential for great love. Yes, there could be various reasons why healing has taken place. However, I know it has been more than human intervention: the grace of God."

"Teresa, I too know of a sorrowful story that occurred during the Holocaust. In a Nazi concentration camp, a Jewish prisoner of war, a doctor who loved God, was faced with an atrocious situation. The Nazis were performing diabolical scientific experiments on pregnant women in the camp. They were binding the women's legs together during labor, causing death for both the mother and the unborn. As a dying wife becomes a martyr, her family endures the horror of their loved one's death.

"The mother's desperate wail, begging for mercy, hauntingly scares the tiniest bird away, sensitive to her heartbreak. It was as if Herod rose from the dead. Due to these dreadful events, many women would approach the doctor when they found themselves pregnant to request an abortion. The doctor, in great anguish, prays to God to help her decide. She has been given the gifts to become a doctor and may save at least the mother's life, but she never became a doctor to perform abortions.

"Furthermore, she knew the mothers wanted the babies, but both would suffer a horrific death. She considers all aspects and weeps to beg for God's help. She decides to complete the abortions. Teresa, was that the wrong decision?"

Teresa's anguish is visible as she cries, "I don't know!"

"Teresa, that is the right answer!"

"What?"

"You don't know. You are not a judge or jury. The decision is God's, not yours or others'. Hobson's choice is best dealt with by God. When human beings try to legislate such matters, they may be preventing people from asking for help from God. The Holy Spirit has the necessary prudence in these matters. Teresa, there is a fruitful ending to this story. The doctor thought that these women would never want to see her again. The women thought the doctor would not want to see them either. However, surprisingly, after the war, as each woman became pregnant, they went to this doctor to deliver their baby. It brought all such joy. They did not expect a welcome from each other; they did not expect an exceptional exception."

The older man is quietly watching and waiting. Teresa is courageous now, a wiser woman, acknowledging how she can help carry the crosses of so many suffering lambs. Teresa feels a flood of gratitude toward God for helping her bear witness to his magnificent love for his children. She looks at the teacher suspiciously, wondering if he can see the thoughts running through her mind, and she glances at him with a questioning look. He appears to want to avoid the suspicious glance.

"Teresa, you know what marks moments of perfect trust? Whenever you feel gratitude and give glory to God—that, my dear woman, is perfect trust."

"So, we achieve perfect trust when we are full of gratitude, suggesting a full recognition of his infinite love. I suppose, when souls can achieve that all the time, they have perfect peace and freedom to love the Lord their God with their whole heart, soul, and mind. Wow, weren't we on a less heavy topic a few minutes ago? Wait a minute, didn't you ask me about Christmas socks?"

He laughs. "Why did he wear the socks at the funeral?"

"His aunt never forgot him, and she loves him. He returns the gift of love by remembering her every Christmas."

"Yes, and God loves his children no matter what decisions they make even though he warns them that it will take them in a more painful direction. God gives his children life and free will. He wants to see a change of heart. He wants to see people have free will, even if his children sometimes make decisions that are not helping their souls and hurt them. Love is patient, and love is kind."

"It reminds me of the story of the prodigal son."

Teresa reflects that we cannot end suffering just through legislation. It may cause more damage. Even with new legislation, which tries to force women to stop having abortions or demand people to pay for all abortions, both sides feel controlled, misunderstood, unloved, judged, and angry. The situation creates an illusion of choice without a choice, namely Hobson's

Choice, which is the same choice frequently faced by abused children. Also, people are not consistent. Some say they are pro-life but also support the death penalty. Some are pro-choice but do not support death with dignity or the legalization of suicide. During biblical times, one side was protecting religious freedom by fighting against the Romans, and another side was rebelling against taxation and oppression. Religious laws and Roman laws could not solve the problems of that day.

Teresa comments, "Each side tries to pull Jesus into the conflict. Why does he stay out of politics? 'My kingdom is not of this world.' People often believe they can create a perfect world without God, without the truth and the law of God. There is an absence of humility before God and others. Politics is the devil's playground. In the garden of Eden, the devil says that God does not want them to eat from the tree because doing so will make them equal to him in power—all-knowing and proud. The 'all-knowing' voices in politics stop listening to their siblings because they think they have all the answers, and they stop asking questions. They believe that they can end human suffering. Is that even a goal that a human being should have while in the temporal plane? Faith conquers the world, not politics. They belong to the world; accordingly, their teachings belong to the world, and the world listens to them. Change occurs by softening each heart tenderly, lovingly, and patiently as Jesus does. Sadly, such exchanges rarely occur in politics because their goals are about power, control, and the arrogance of believing that only one side knows what is right and the other side is stupid.

"Teacher, there are too many teachers and no students. Only God can perfectly balance the common good and individual rights. Humans will never have the complete picture while here on earth. It is because we do not understand the purpose of suffering as Jesus did. We need help but do not ask for it because of our pride. Some argue 'some good comes out of politics,' but I think of the temptations of Christ during the forty days in the desert, where the devil was entirely political with his suggestions. He frequently does that, a little truth in a lie or a little good in evil like many politicians of this day. When something good comes out of politics, it comes from the humility of heart and grace. For example, the school lunch program, started by the Children's Aid Society of New York. Some say Jesus was a politician—that is a lie. Diplomacy and prudence may appear that way to those who value politics over the truths of the spirit, the laws of God. 'The Lord, your God, shall you worship and him alone shall you serve.' His rules are different from those of man; they appear peculiar. However, those who love Jesus trust his truth and his laws." As a contemplative, Teresa quietly considers the following.

His Truth will set us free, "I am the truth and the light"

Do not count on your fears, your anxiety,

"Oh, foolish people, look to the mercy of God and his Divinity"

Jesus, I trust in you

Do not trust in yourself, your poor decisions, and your ego driven plans,

"Oh, lost sheep of Israel, look to the will of God—

the Truth, the Light and the Way"

Jesus, I trust in you

Do not trust other people because they are like you, they are sinful

"Oh, my children-Trust in me, I am with you always"

Jesus, I trust in you

You alone, you my love, my life and my All.

ALTIERO, 1998

===============

"Teresa, Tom loves his aunt with all her peculiarities. They may not see eye to eye, but he does not doubt her love, and he trusts it entirely. If the children of God learn to love God that way and trust in his good judgment, they will find peace, truth, and joy not of this world, as Peter did when he was asked, 'But Peter do you love me?'

"Teresa, do you find me peculiar, as Tom found his aunt?"

"Yes, in an adorable way," she teases.

He laughs with joy. "Teresa, there are two parts to a gift. The giving and receiving. You must trust someone to accept their offer and their intentions. It often takes time, as it did for Tom and as it did in the serious examples you and I have discussed today. You can offer a gift, but it only becomes a gift when accepted, as you will soon see, when you learn about little Edith."

Chapter Twenty-Seven

Lessons of Love

Edith is a three-year-old girl who notices the lovely dandelions down the block in the field by her house for the first time. They are beautiful, all soft and fluffy like the clouds in the sky. The first person Edith thinks of, as the recipient of this beautiful gift, is her mother. So, with building excitement, she gathers a bunch in her hand. The little girl hides them behind her back. If her mother is looking out the window, it will spoil the fun.

She runs home as fast as she can. Little does she know that the flowering treasures are being taken away by the wind because of the gentle spring breeze and her relentless pace. When she arrives at her front door, she rings the doorbell, and her mother opens the door. Edith then exclaims in glee, "Mommy, I picked some beautiful flowers for you." Then, Edith thrusts her little hand upwards only to see in horror some bare stems, and she begins to cry.

Quickly, her mother grasps the items with joy and gratefully sings, "Oh, my! These are beautiful, and I will put them in a glass on the kitchen table right now. How did you know I was looking for such a centerpiece? What beautiful green stems!" Of course, by now, little Edith is both happy and amazed by her mother's reaction. Next week, her mother will be surprised when she gets the entire flower home. As Edith gets older, she always remembers to buy her mother gifts because she feels terrific when she does so.

The older man proffers a question, "Teresa, how do you feel when you give a gift that is graciously accepted and appreciated? Are you more likely to provide the person with more gifts when they show gratitude?" These questions sound just rhetorical, so Teresa waits for the teacher to continue. "If God is the creator of all and the greatest gift is your life, how could you show gratitude for the gift of life?"

"I should live life well and spend it glorifying God, who is all good and deserving of all my love. In glorifying God, I am free to love and love again."

With this, the old man begins to joyfully cry and gratefully exclaims, "Yes, this is true; this is true, my dear little lamb."

Teresa puts her hand on his shoulder and looks at him with great love.

He then says, "If simple acts of love are what is of great value within the creator's kingdom, it could be that they are treasures of priceless value, held within the human heart. This precious jewel of the soul—and sharing it with others—is acknowledged with great approval from heaven. So, whether you are a seamstress or a tailor, let compassion be the thread of your needle to help mend broken hearts.

"Lessons of Love. They are so simple."

Maggie and Mike are watching Teresa from afar. They have numerous hypotheses about what and who is her conversation partner on the bench. Still, since they cannot see the person, they sometimes assume that she is an actress rehearsing her lines. Then again, the couple recalls seeing a significantly older man. Mike is inattentive, and at first, Maggie just ignores his distraction; he is a scientist lost in his thoughts. She puts the binoculars into her eyes again. Why is the girl raising her arm as if someone is on the bench with her? Does she have an imaginary friend? Is this the friend to whom she is saying goodbye today? Her husband is persistently tapping Maggie on the shoulder.

"Crap, Mike, what is it now? It can't be more important than what I am watching." Mike persists. She lowers her binoculars. Mike is pointing at the sky. Maggie's jaw drops in amazement, "What the heck is that?"

Teresa is continuing her conversation with the teacher, "You say that a gift needs both a giver and receiver. On both ends of that equation is free will. We must choose to give, and another must choose to accept with gratitude. You have also said that love is a choice. So, it is also a gift, is that true?"

The teacher turns to Teresa, taking both her hands in his, and earnestly states, "Love comes from God. He gives infinite love to his children. You can choose to accept it and return it. Love is a choice. Love, my dear, is the exceptional exception." They sit together in silence until the teacher stands up, indicating that it is time to leave. Teresa does not stand up; she is hoping he will sit back down.

"Teresa, if you met Jesus again, will you recognize him?"

"Of course."

"How will you know?"

"I saw him in a dream, and—"

The teacher frowns and sternly states. "That was a gift!" The teacher has never been cross with her. How could she be so arrogant? "What if you did not recognize him?"

Now Teresa begins to shake and tremble; the thought of not recognizing Jesus terrifies her. "That would be horrible!"

The teacher turns his back and starts to walk away, but pauses. "But why would it be terrible?"

She exclaims in tears, "Because I love him, I love him!"

The teacher begins to walk again and then pauses again. "Then, you will know him." He takes a couple of steps forward.

Teresa is still hysterical, and he is now two yards away. "Are you sure? Are you sure?"

He seems not to hear her, but suddenly the sky opens, and a great light falls from the sky upon him. He turns around to look at her, but he looks different, much younger and dressed in tunic and sandals. He has the face of a man who would give his life for you, a sacred human. He tilts his head and smiles. "You will know him. You will know him by your heart." Smiling with great love, he ascends into a great light.

"It is you! It is you! You have been here all along. My heart sings, and my soul sees. My Jesus! Oh, Holy One, you are the Exceptional Exception!"

Chapter Twenty-Eight

In the Park

You may be wondering what Mike and Maggie are doing. Well, they see the entire thing, and yes, that is for another day and another story!
Please meet me in the park someday. I love the company.

www.ingramcontent.com/pod-product-compliance
Lightning Source LLC
Chambersburg PA
CBHW071132250626
47159CB00006B/2206